Christmas Stories

From the Crones Castle

by

Patsy Stanley

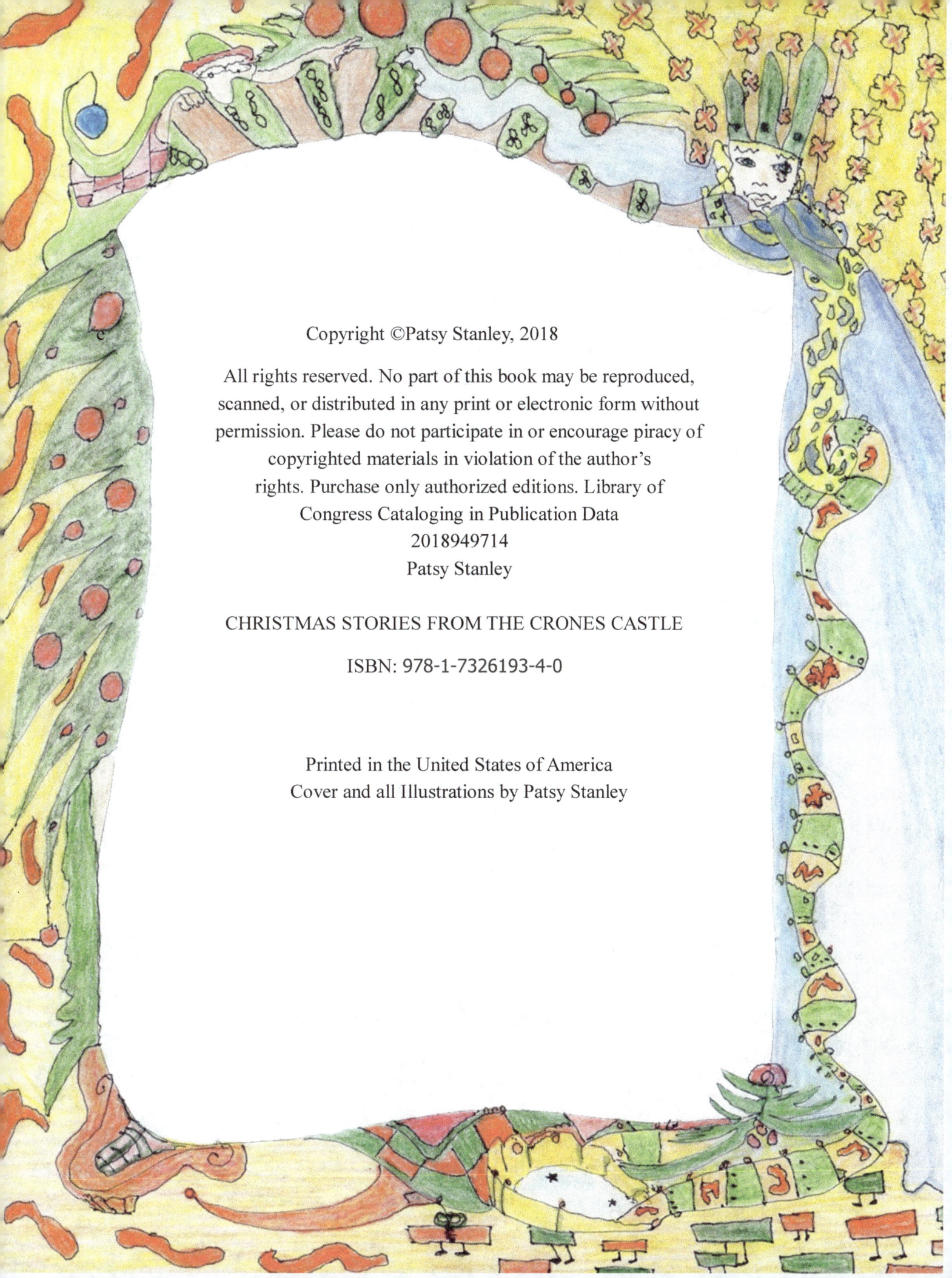

Library of
Congress Cataloging in Publication Data
2018949714
Patsy Stanley

CHRISTMAS STORIES FROM THE CRONES CASTLE

ISBN: 978-1-7326193-4-0

Printed in the United States of America
Cover and all Illustrations by Patsy Stanley

Table of Contents

The Kingdom of True Believer in Imagination
and its inhabitants…
the Crones, the Box Keepers, and Others…

T'was in the ancient days of long ago,
before the time of the Speaking,
when children came from far and near,
to claim the land they were seeking…

Long ago, three orders of Magi living near the northernmost corner of the heavens were minding their own business when all of a sudden, they were sent on a mission to Earth. They were sent to build the Kingdom of True Believers in Imagination for one reason and one reason only; to protect children from dream stealers, want removers, and hope hiders, of which there were many. The three orders of Magi would stay and rule the new Kingdom and try to make certain that the children who came to Earth might keep the dreams that lived in on their imagination.

Only then could each child share in the language of everything that exists… real and imagined.

The three orders of Magi, known as the Box Keepers, the Crones, and the Others, knew this was a critical mission. They searched until they located a rusty, old, abandoned shoe box factory in a vacant lot on the edge of a big city. The moment they found it, they danced the tango and hurried inside; soon they had built their new Kingdom for children. They left the outside of the rusty, old, abandoned shoe box factory just as it was and probably had been nearly forever; for it was an excellent disguise. No one would ever suspect there was a magic Kingdom hidden inside such an old, lonely-colored factory.

1

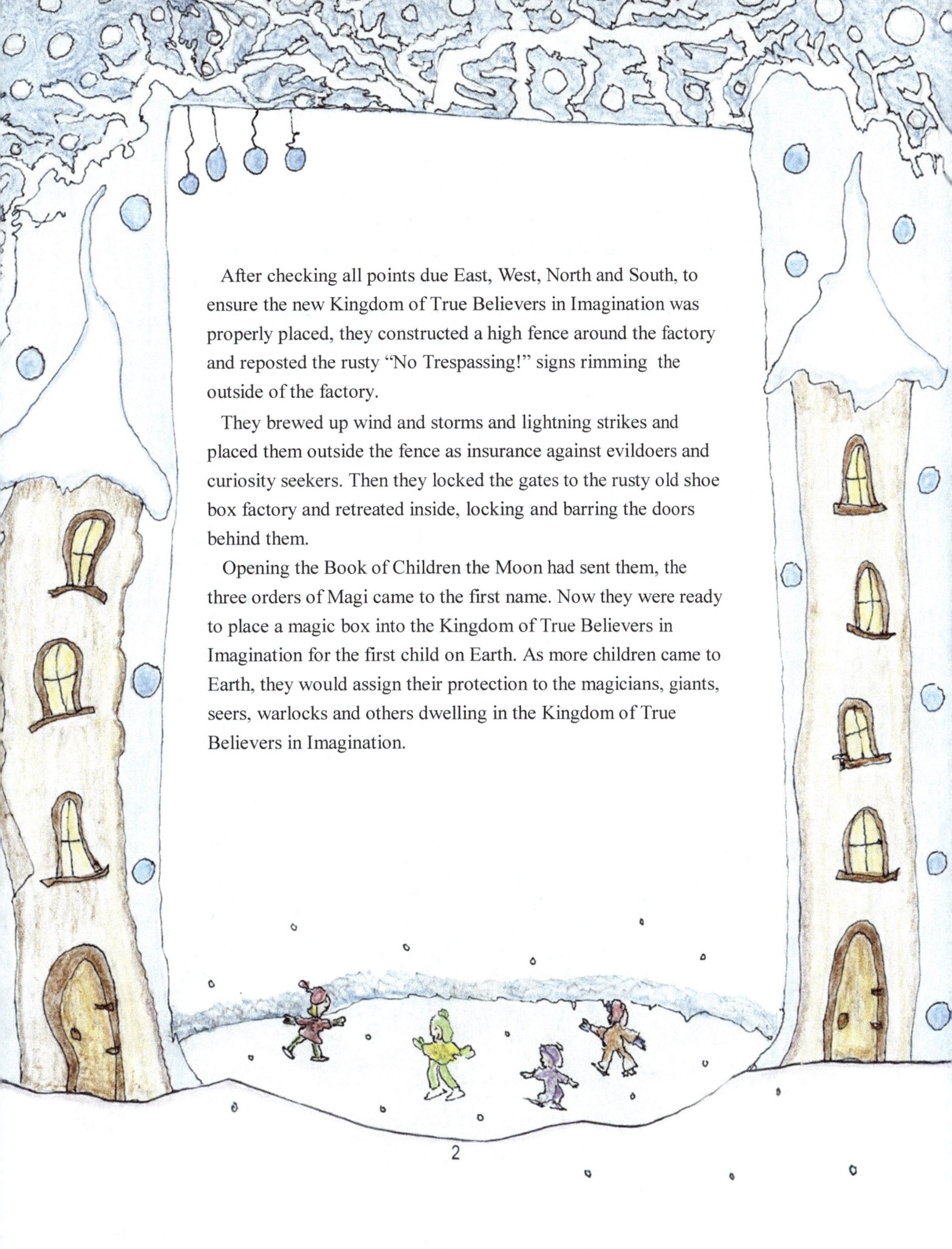

After checking all points due East, West, North and South, to ensure the new Kingdom of True Believers in Imagination was properly placed, they constructed a high fence around the factory and reposted the rusty "No Trespassing!" signs rimming the outside of the factory.

They brewed up wind and storms and lightning strikes and placed them outside the fence as insurance against evildoers and curiosity seekers. Then they locked the gates to the rusty old shoe box factory and retreated inside, locking and barring the doors behind them.

Opening the Book of Children the Moon had sent them, the three orders of Magi came to the first name. Now they were ready to place a magic box into the Kingdom of True Believers in Imagination for the first child on Earth. As more children came to Earth, they would assign their protection to the magicians, giants, seers, warlocks and others dwelling in the Kingdom of True Believers in Imagination.

From that ancient beginning, clear through this very moment, all of Earth's children have had, and will always have, their own magic box kept safe in the Kingdom hidden inside the old shoebox factory.

Indeed, they are kept safe in the magic, secret factory residing in a covenanted location near the merriest measures of rounded Earth, not far north of the- shiver me timbers!- boardwalk at the Emerald Port, where the masts of pirate ships sail the blue seas, their tall masts brushing the tops of white clouds.

Every child knows about their magic box and all the other magic boxes resting on shelves and in all the nooks and crannies children secretly share. Inside each child's magic box dwell ogres and moans, cool, sweet songs, rhymes and riddles, and mysterious smells. Children fill their magic boxes with sea shells, rocks and grass, and ransom notes from pirates' coves. They place hopes and dreams and laughter, and many long, silent moments in them.

As children grow up, ribbons and rings and baseballs and other things replace the first things in their magic boxes. But time passes, as it always does, sometimes slow and sometimes fast, and the children grow up.
They set aside their magic boxes and forget all about them. They go out in the world and find an ordinary box factory of some kind or another, where everyday things are made, and go to work.

4

Oh well…but wait!…There were and are, and always will be, some children who grow up and never forget about their sea shells and rocks and ribbons and things. Those grownups can see the magic boxes hidden in the shadows of a child's room, looking plain and dull and not very important to the other grownups around them.

And so it is, and was, and always will be. The children and the grownups who never forget, share the forgotten wisdom of magic box keeping with the Box Keepers, the Crones, and the Others who dwell in the Kingdom of True Believers in Imagination; the Kingdom hidden inside the old shoe box factory. Together, they keep the vigil each time the notes, noises, songs, and dreams fade from a child's memory; they keep the vigils and the songs of the magic self and save them for a rainy day.

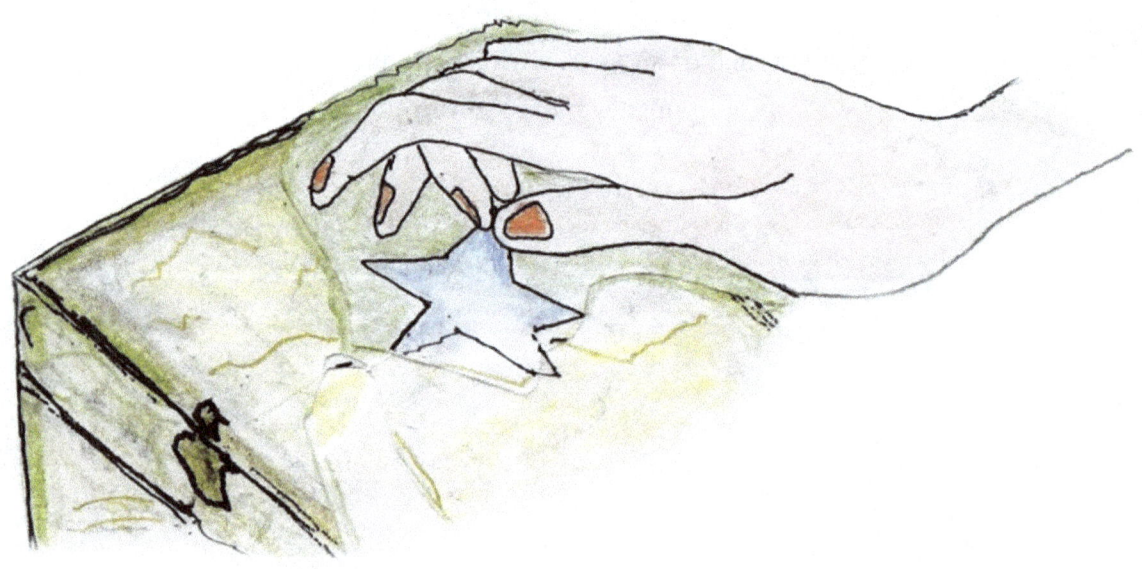

The Box Keepers

Box Keepers are strong, stalwart, and dedicated. They travel back and forth between the Kingdom and the children and are on call night and day. Much training is required to become a Box Keeper, for they are sent out on very important quests. They learn to sit straight and ride hard and to get there on time. They love their horses and the sound of creaking leather. They love magic and mysteries and baked beans and biscuits. But most of all, they love the child that lives within each and everyone.

Each Box Keeper carries their own magic box with them.
Some boxes hold robin eggs, blue tail feathers from the
bird that rolls in the dust, and bronze pebbles. Others carry
hard boiled facts and tiger roars that speed up the
development of attributes.

At the bottom of each their magic boxes lives a funny
bone named after a famous detective, like "Slam Shade.".
Each funny bone lives close to the subway station at 77
Magic Street, until it learns its way around the highways
and byways of the Three Lyrical Wisdoms, Humor,
Discernment, and Discretion. Out of this learning comes
hats with feathers, capes and boots, songs and ballads, and
the refined art of road sign reading.

Box Keepers are sent out on quests. They ride through
dust and drought, through rain and sleet and over high hills
and down steep valleys. They ride through vales and gales
and monsoons, but mostly they ride through trial and error
and sometimes, terror.

After training, each Box Keepers is sent to the Crones' castle
to learn about the Silver Webs.

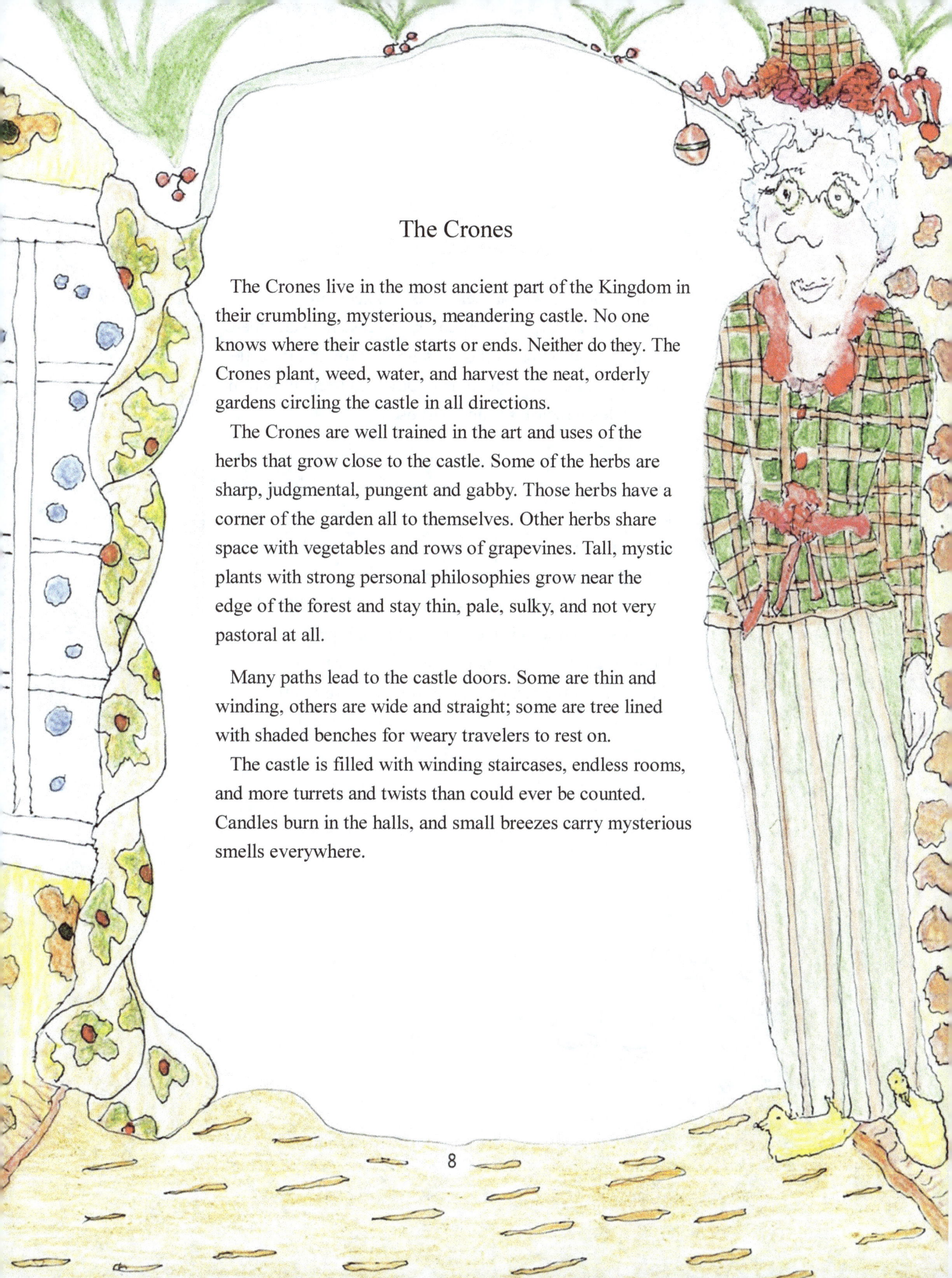

The Crones

The Crones live in the most ancient part of the Kingdom in their crumbling, mysterious, meandering castle. No one knows where their castle starts or ends. Neither do they. The Crones plant, weed, water, and harvest the neat, orderly gardens circling the castle in all directions.

The Crones are well trained in the art and uses of the herbs that grow close to the castle. Some of the herbs are sharp, judgmental, pungent and gabby. Those herbs have a corner of the garden all to themselves. Other herbs share space with vegetables and rows of grapevines. Tall, mystic plants with strong personal philosophies grow near the edge of the forest and stay thin, pale, sulky, and not very pastoral at all.

Many paths lead to the castle doors. Some are thin and winding, others are wide and straight; some are tree lined with shaded benches for weary travelers to rest on.

The castle is filled with winding staircases, endless rooms, and more turrets and twists than could ever be counted. Candles burn in the halls, and small breezes carry mysterious smells everywhere.

The Crones go about their tasks and keep order in the castle with a sharp word of common sense here and there. Their wisdom and steadfastness flows through the castle like cool water on a hot summer day, and keep all within the castle on their tasks and purposes.

The Crones keep the elves and trolls sorting moss and disappearing under bridges at just the right moment. They keep the giants pondering and the fairies in flight. They keep the Wails and Moans from wandering around the castle and fading in and out of every room.

Grumpy sighs play Canasta. Shouts and shrieks hold contests to see who is the loudest. Small breezes unfurl banners and march along the tops of the castle walls while they wait for the call of a child to find its way to them.

The Silver Webs

The Crones mine the Silver Webs from the Moon. On full Moon nights, the Crones take their baskets and gather in a field near the castle and chant and sing ancient songs. Their tunes and lyrics float high into the sky, attracting the attention of the little moonbeams that light the Moon's path across the night sky. Little moonbeams are always a very curious bunch, so some of them drift down to hear the songs better. But the closer they get to Earth, the heavier they become. They feel themselves sinking, closing their eyes and falling asleep before they drop and plop to the ground.

The Crones gather the tiny, shiny pieces of
sleeping silver into their baskets and carry them
to the vesting Crones waiting in the castle's
ritual rooms. The vesting Crones spread out the
sleeping silver moonbeams on long tables.

Almost as one, they "ooh" and "aahhh" and chuckle
over each tiny, shiny silver circle. They massage and
stretch each one and weave them into silver webs.
They take the Silver Webs for walks; they rock them,
and sing songs to them of amazing, unusual
possibilities that have never been thought of before.

On dark, clear nights, they carry the Silver Webs
outside under the shining stars. The vesting Crones
fling the Webs up to the sky, so they can get
acquainted with their Elders, the Moon and Stars.

When each Silver Web is well-infused with just the
right amount of particles of stardust and Earth matter,
they rest on the shelves of the ritual rooms near the
castle kitchens.

Shadows and curves dance across the gleaming Silver Webs. Mysterious smells curl around them but hurry off when a Crone shoos them away. Each day the Silver Webs listen to the sounds of chants and proper magic spells mixed with the bangs and clangs of pots and pans. They sniff the good, sensible smell of soup from the nearby kitchens or bread from the bustling bakery.

They stay content as the chants and spells, bangs and clangs, and smells pass their way, for they know that someday, a Crone will come for them and send them out on a quest with a Box Keeper, and on that quest, they will meet their very own child. They rest in orderly rows on their shelves in the ritual rooms, shimmering in serene silence while waiting for that day.

The Seasons

The seasons come and go in the Kingdom hidden inside the rusty, old, abandoned shoe box factory, just as they do everywhere else on Earth. Spring came, and the water bubbled and ran over pebbles. It spoke of running through jungles and of wandering along mossy creek banks. The water told tales of turquoise seas and mermaids living in warm, tropical oceans. It spoke of the stern gray northern seas, filled year 'round with glaciers, noise, and cold. The water described warming the shores of many lands, and running up on beaches to cleanse itself in the fine, white sand.

Summer followed spring with dancing, snapping fire that told stories of dark nights, with people circled around it, speaking strange languages, cooking food over it and warming themselves at its flames. Summer fire spoke of keeping vigils and providing light for lost people. Fire was always hungry; it told tales of the smallness of campfires in night deserts, and of the great, roaring fires of feasts people often enjoyed in cool, deep forests.

13

Fall told tales of kites streaming high above the Earth and of playing with clouds. Fall worked hardest just before winter came, scaling bark and blowing red, orange, and yellow leaves off the trees, drying the tall grasses, and bending them over the ground. Fall puffed out its cheeks and danced and swirled the hot dust of summer into cool, thin circles, readying the Earth once more for winter.

Winter chilled the air and layered snow everywhere. The snow blanketed many of the world's faults, at least for a time. Winter's cold and snow covered the land, so it could rest until spring came once again.

The Christmas Gathering

Winter lay claim to the land. Time passed, and Christmas drew near. All those living in the Kingdom of True Believers in Imagination hidden inside the old, abandoned, shoe box factory, the Crones, Box Keepers, and Others got busy preparing for the Yuletide.

The tall Christmas tree stood in the Great Hall, its needles and branches waiting for decorations. Bells, herbs, and dried flowers waited to be spread across the mantels and around the windows. Plum puddings, cakes, nuts, and all manner of gilded fruit rested in the kitchen pantries, letting all their flavors deepen and sweeten. Their tantalizing aromas wafted throughout the castle.

Christmas was proceeding as usual. That is, until a Green Seer's sneeze echoed through the castle halls, rattling the dishes and knocking silverware off the tables.

It was rare to have a Green Seer pass near the castle, for they lived far away in Folgoth Woods. The Green Seers were rarely seen by anybody, no matter what or where they passed, because they were oracles with divine insight and terribly shy.

The Green Seers did not like to leave Folgoth Woods, for they were the Guardians of the gifts of Peace. There were many parts to Peace, both small and large. The Green Seers protected them all, hiding each one under layers of the stern, all knowing Dust of Ages in Folgoth Woods, a place no one else dared enter without permission.

Now, as you can imagine, there are many other kinds of dust in this world, and it is true that dust has covered many a curious thing. There is gold dust, for which many a good prospector digs and pans. There is lonesome, wandering dust laying around houses until it is shooed away. House dust is cousin to desert dust, which has Star and Moon dust for its Elders. Those three windy cousins tend to join each other in infinite dancing patterns and wander wherever they take a notion to.

Yes. There are all kinds of dust. Then there is the Sandman, who sprinkles magic dust to give little children good dreams.

But long before any of those Dusts came along, the Dust of Ages was layering itself over Peace, protecting it, traveling with it. The Green Seers had guarded Peace ever since the Dust of Ages had chosen Folgoth Woods to settle down in. The trees in Folgoth Woods were short and newly green when the Dust out of which everything comes and to which everything returns, chose it.

The Dust of Ages settled in and mixed in with the green of Folgoth Woods. That is how the Green Seers got assigned their name. Their number one job was overseeing the Dust of Ages that hid the gifts of Peace.

The Crones, Box Keepers and Others knew that if a Green Seer sneezed near them, it meant they had a chance at receiving a gift of Peace, large or small, for Christmas. They dropped what they were doing and ran to find the Green Seer. They searched until they stood on the edge of Folgoth Woods. Ringing the edge of the ancient, deep, dark forest stood rows of bones and stones engraved with the names of Seers and Guardians of Folgoth Woods.

They froze, still and silent, until Elder Silverado Foggy Fitz and began speaking aloud the names on the bone and stone markers.

As soon as she spoke the last name, they heard a Green Seer's sneeze echo through the dark forest. That was their signal of approval.

Foggy Fitz led the way through Folgoth Woods. Finally she stopped and pointed to a small, dusty bundle hidden in the hollow of a tree so old that most of it had crumbled to dust.

She took a silver web from a pocket and unraveled most of it into a thin, long silver cord. Then she tossed the rest of the silver web over the bundle and pulled it tight. She turned and hurried back through the forest, unwinding the silver cord in her hands as she went.

Soon, they stood outside the gloomy forest once more. Foggy Fitz began naming the Guardians of Folgoth Woods again, asking for permission to carry away the bundle of Peace. Each time she spoke a name, the silver cord loosened and she drew it tight again.

The rest set up camp and built a small platform to lay the bundle on. The gardening Crones shook out their capes and tossed them across the platform, covering it with a bed of wild sweet grass and forget me nots. The Others gathered moss and speckled fern eggs to pack around the bundle.

Then they waited, for they knew that all Dust is the slow accumulation of the past, of lives lived and essences of lessons learned. They knew that Dust didn't have a speck of time left in it, one way or another, so it didn't care one bit about how long it took to get anywhere. It didn't have to answer to time any more. It would show up when it was ready, and for its own reasons.

19

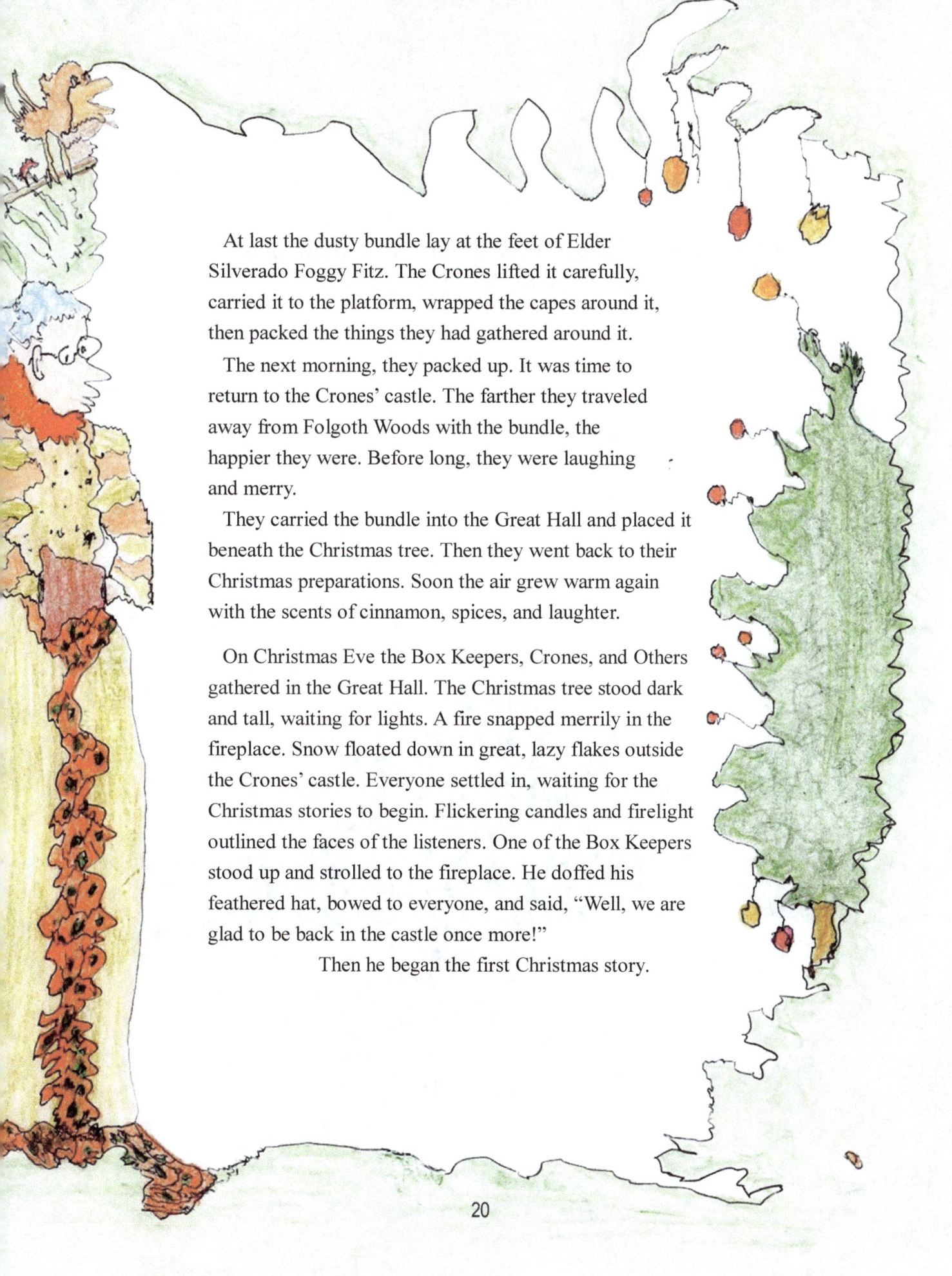

At last the dusty bundle lay at the feet of Elder Silverado Foggy Fitz. The Crones lifted it carefully, carried it to the platform, wrapped the capes around it, then packed the things they had gathered around it.

The next morning, they packed up. It was time to return to the Crones' castle. The farther they traveled away from Folgoth Woods with the bundle, the happier they were. Before long, they were laughing and merry.

They carried the bundle into the Great Hall and placed it beneath the Christmas tree. Then they went back to their Christmas preparations. Soon the air grew warm again with the scents of cinnamon, spices, and laughter.

On Christmas Eve the Box Keepers, Crones, and Others gathered in the Great Hall. The Christmas tree stood dark and tall, waiting for lights. A fire snapped merrily in the fireplace. Snow floated down in great, lazy flakes outside the Crones' castle. Everyone settled in, waiting for the Christmas stories to begin. Flickering candles and firelight outlined the faces of the listeners. One of the Box Keepers stood up and strolled to the fireplace. He doffed his feathered hat, bowed to everyone, and said, "Well, we are glad to be back in the castle once more!"

Then he began the first Christmas story.

1 The Small and Smelly Wizard who Knew Odor was in the Nose of the Smeller

Once upon a time, a stubborn and wordy little wizard attending the Whipstitch School of Wizardry wouldn't bathe. Days, weeks and months passed. The little wizard grew so smelly he no longer noticed his own smelliness, but he still sniffed happily at strong-smelling cheeses, especially pecorinos.

At last, the exhausted headmasters of the Whipstitch School declared that enough was enough. After much muttering, arguing, and nose plugging, they decided to banish the smelly, stubborn little wizard.

In whispered legend, there existed a hidden map leading to a desert oasis no one had ever returned from. They began a frantic search for that long lost map.

The headmasters took this desperate action out of a profound premonition of what they and others would, no doubt, experience from the smells emitting from the little wizard. He wouldn't bathe. Not now, not today, not yesterday, and never more.

The headmaster's desperate search for the secret map of the legendary desert had not been easy; just to steal the map from the belfry of a rival school in a faraway land had taken all their combined skills.

They stole the map in the deep, dark of night. Fleeing home, they hastily lit a lamp and pored over the map's contents until they discovered the location of the hidden desert oasis. They smiled at each other in relief and shouted, "Aha!"

But time was of the essence. They most certainly had to hurry. When daybreak came, the little wizard would once again discharge into the air even more pungent, swirling, sour secretions. They knew this well from past experience.

They roused the sleepy little wizard from his bed, and without any reservations or troublesome, nagging sympathy, promptly teleported him to the desert and left him there, along with many shouted instructions on the importance of bathing.

The transport required seven headmasters, twelve protective spells, three scented handkerchiefs, and a level of concentrated magic rarely seen outside of dragon emergencies.

The exhausted headmasters rubbed their eyes, yawned, and went off to sleep the peaceful sleep of the just. They had every reason to believe the smelly little wizard was now a former student of the famous Whipstitch School of Wizardry…

The little wizard landed in the sandy desert, and promptly fell asleep again. The next morning, he woke up to the sound of elderberry trees quarreling above him, and a gabbling, dabbling, little purple stream running through the sandy desert surrounding him. Astounded, he jumped to his feet. He shouted, "I'm in a desert? How did I get here? Who did this to me?"

And so, the little wizards' sojourn in the mostly forgotten little desert oasis began. It was hot in the desert, so very soon after he arrived, the stinky, mummy smelling, dry little wizard changed his mind about bathing.

He decided to bathe in the dabbling, little purple stream. In a most fateful moment of discovery, he swaggered over to the stream and tried to stick his toe in it.

To his surprise, the little purple stream rolled smoothly out of his reach. His foot landed on hot, dry sand. Astounded, he tried again. It took many tries before the little wizard realized the pottering, puttering, dabbling little purple stream that, in fact, changed to many attractive shades of lavender and lilac, wasn't going to let him have any of its water, forcing him to remain a small and rancid wizard full of weeks and weeks of reeks.

Near the pottering, puttering, dabbling little purple stream stood a grove of elderberry trees that quarreled with each other all day long. They had been planted there by a mighty mystic.

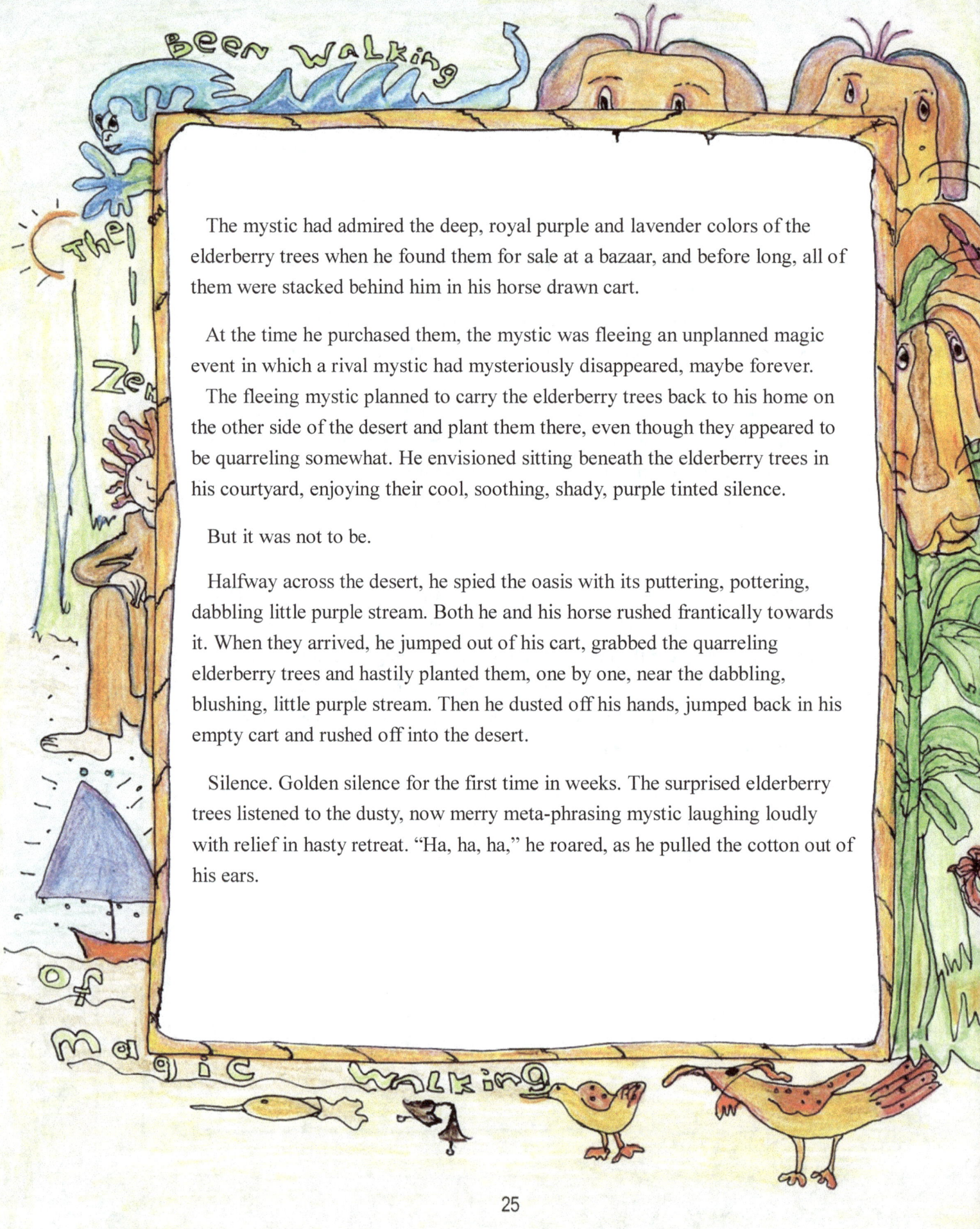

The mystic had admired the deep, royal purple and lavender colors of the elderberry trees when he found them for sale at a bazaar, and before long, all of them were stacked behind him in his horse drawn cart.

At the time he purchased them, the mystic was fleeing an unplanned magic event in which a rival mystic had mysteriously disappeared, maybe forever.

The fleeing mystic planned to carry the elderberry trees back to his home on the other side of the desert and plant them there, even though they appeared to be quarreling somewhat. He envisioned sitting beneath the elderberry trees in his courtyard, enjoying their cool, soothing, shady, purple tinted silence.

But it was not to be.

Halfway across the desert, he spied the oasis with its puttering, pottering, dabbling little purple stream. Both he and his horse rushed frantically towards it. When they arrived, he jumped out of his cart, grabbed the quarreling elderberry trees and hastily planted them, one by one, near the dabbling, blushing, little purple stream. Then he dusted off his hands, jumped back in his empty cart and rushed off into the desert.

Silence. Golden silence for the first time in weeks. The surprised elderberry trees listened to the dusty, now merry meta-phrasing mystic laughing loudly with relief in hasty retreat. "Ha, ha, ha," he roared, as he pulled the cotton out of his ears.

The elderberry trees watched the mystic until he disappeared into the distant, burning sands. Then they turned to each other and embarked on another round of quarreling.

The little wizard and the elderberry trees were always hot, and it was all the fault of the pottering, puttering, dabbling little purple stream that wouldn't let them have any water.

Each day, while the hot sun shone down on the desert, the small and rancid wizard sweated greatly and cast many spells against the little purple stream. The babbling little stream ignored him and instead, practiced changing to shades of purple, eggplant and orchid.

Sometimes the little wizard scowled and prowled back and forth under the quarreling elderberry trees. Waving his arms and jumping up and down, the little wizard joined in, making dire predictions and peppery points that mostly didn't have anything to do with the deeper subjects the elderberry trees liked discussing.

When they grew tired of the stinky little wizard, they put their knobby roots and hard toes to good use. In other words, they kicked him out.

Time passed in the little, lost, almost forgotten, desert oasis until Christmas drew near again. The elderberry trees decided to discuss pressing matters: why they had been given the task of putting up with a small, and by then, very smelly wizard; and why the pottering, puttering, dabbling little purple stream at their feet would give them no water.

Their voices grew louder and louder. They were enjoying themselves immensely when the smelly, small and rancid wizard strode into their midst and shouted, "Stop!"

The elderberry trees stopped quarreling and drew themselves up. Silence fell among them as they caught their breaths. They lifted their branches as high as they could, striving for less aromatic air than the little wizard's presence carried. The little wizard shouted into the silence, "Christmas should be extinct!"

They shouted back at him, "Extinct? Does that mean you are going to take a bath?"

The elderberry trees started laughing. The little wizard shook his fist at them and shouted. They watched him stomping around and hollering and were highly entertained for a short time. Then they resumed quarreling among themselves.

The little wizard turned his back on them and swaggered to the bank of the puttering, pottering, dabbling little purple stream. He pointed his finger at it and shouted, "Be still so I can get wet!"

The little purple stream shaded to dark lavender and phlox and ignored him. It had problems of its own. It had many questions for which it had no answers. It wondered why it was purple. It wondered why it changed colors but stayed purple. How did it do that?

Why did it run faster in some places, and slower in others?

How old was it?

When had it been formed?

Where was its mother stream?

How had it got here?

Where did it start, and most importantly, where did it end?...

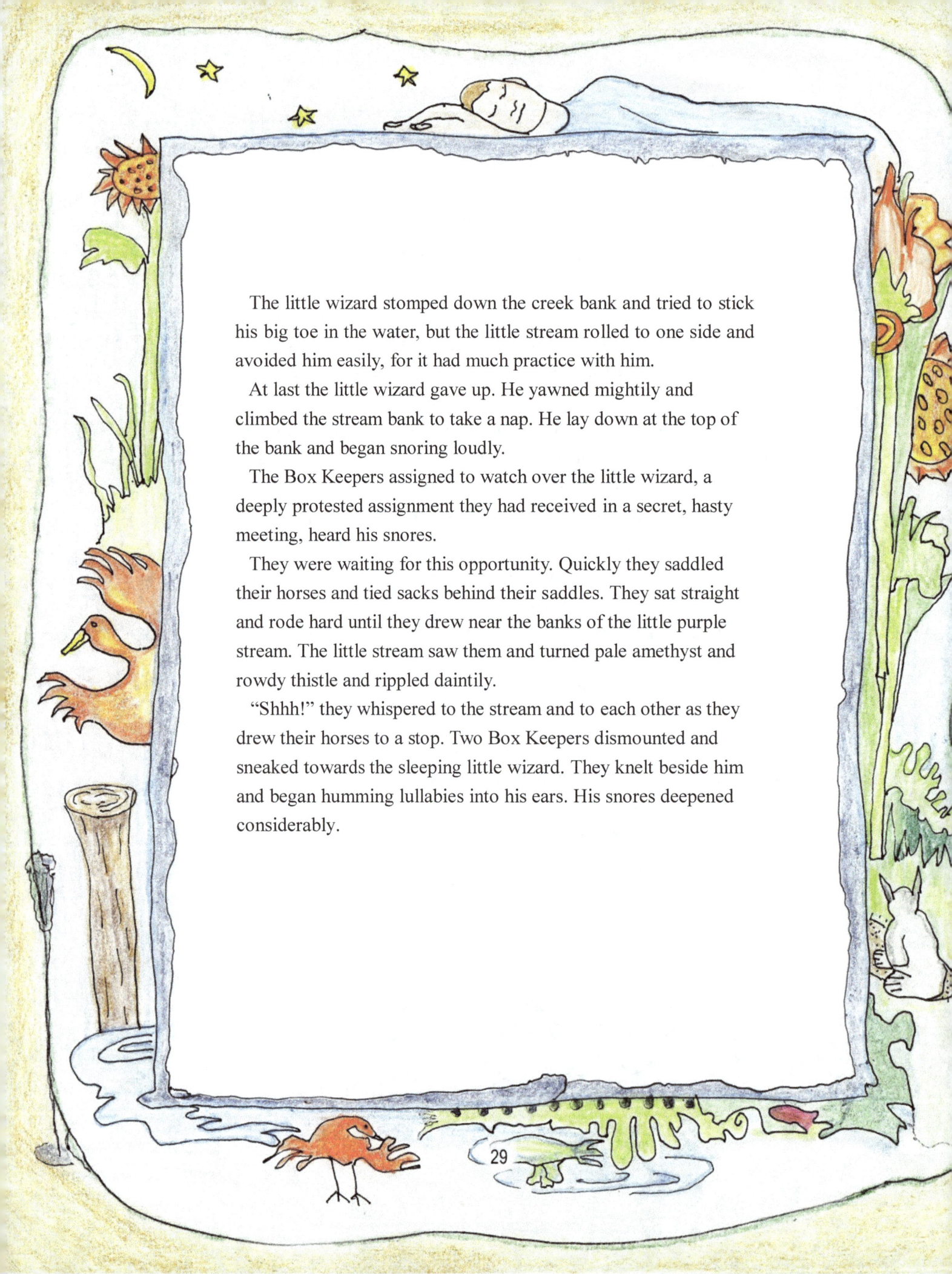

The little wizard stomped down the creek bank and tried to stick his big toe in the water, but the little stream rolled to one side and avoided him easily, for it had much practice with him.

At last the little wizard gave up. He yawned mightily and climbed the stream bank to take a nap. He lay down at the top of the bank and began snoring loudly.

The Box Keepers assigned to watch over the little wizard, a deeply protested assignment they had received in a secret, hasty meeting, heard his snores.

They were waiting for this opportunity. Quickly they saddled their horses and tied sacks behind their saddles. They sat straight and rode hard until they drew near the banks of the little purple stream. The little stream saw them and turned pale amethyst and rowdy thistle and rippled daintily.

"Shhh!" they whispered to the stream and to each other as they drew their horses to a stop. Two Box Keepers dismounted and sneaked towards the sleeping little wizard. They knelt beside him and began humming lullabies into his ears. His snores deepened considerably.

The rest of the Box Keepers untied their sacks and set to work. They spread soft, white sand mixed with small, smooth stones schooled in the wisdoms of the ages along the stream bed. The cool, wise stones began murmuring their stories; after all, being stones, they were older than anyone and anything else there, except maybe the water.

The little stream began rubbing the fresh sand into place and rearranging the stones. It didn't pay any attention to the Box Keepers when they began dipping iris and periwinkle shaded water out of it. It was too busy asking questions and listening to the explanations of the smooth, cool stones.

The stones had needed a student, and the little stream had needed teachers. Together, they happily explored the many questions the little stream had stored up.

The little stream asked, "Why do I change colors?"

It modestly shaded into plum and old lavender, hoping for a reply.

"There are many reasons, including your moods," a stone answered.

Another, older stone spoke up, "As your temperature changes, so do your colors."

"You are young and learning," the oldest stone of all droned soothingly.

"You are many shades of purple because you are in the time of learning not to turn into the vulgar shades of vanity and extravagance."

"But I don't want to be humble," the little stream protested. "I like being vain and extravagant!"

"Don't worry. You will never be humble. You are purple, after all," the stones murmured in harmony.

The elderberry trees were watching the Box Keepers and debating what they were doing. The trees were so busy quarreling with each other that it took them a moment to notice the Box Keeper standing under them.

He was dressed in a fine black tuxedo with tails, his black shoes polished to a mirror shine. A music stand with a stack of music sheets on it stood in front of him. The elderberry trees looked at each other.

"How did he get here?"

"Who is he?"

At the mere thought of more smelly visitors, the trees raised their branches as high as they could and shouted, "Oh no!"

The Box Keeper glared up at them and rapped sharply on his music stand. "Quiet, please!" he roared.

He tossed his large mane of hair back and "aaa-hemmed!" in a deep voice until he had their attention. He fixed them with a steely glare and began to sing in a grand voice, waving his conductor's baton around. He gestured for them to join in. The elderberry trees watched him a moment before turning to each other and putting forth their theories, all at the same time, about what the Box Keeper was doing.

"What does he want from us?"

"Isn't he dressed a little warmly? After all, this IS a desert we're stuck in."

"But maybe he doesn't know that."

"How would he not know that?"

"Does he realize where he is, and on Christmas Eve, of all times?"

"Maybe he was taken to the wrong place by the mystic, just like us," one of them said.

They all began weeping dark shades of magenta and wailing, "We've been waiting for the mystic to return for such a long time! Surely he'll return soon!"

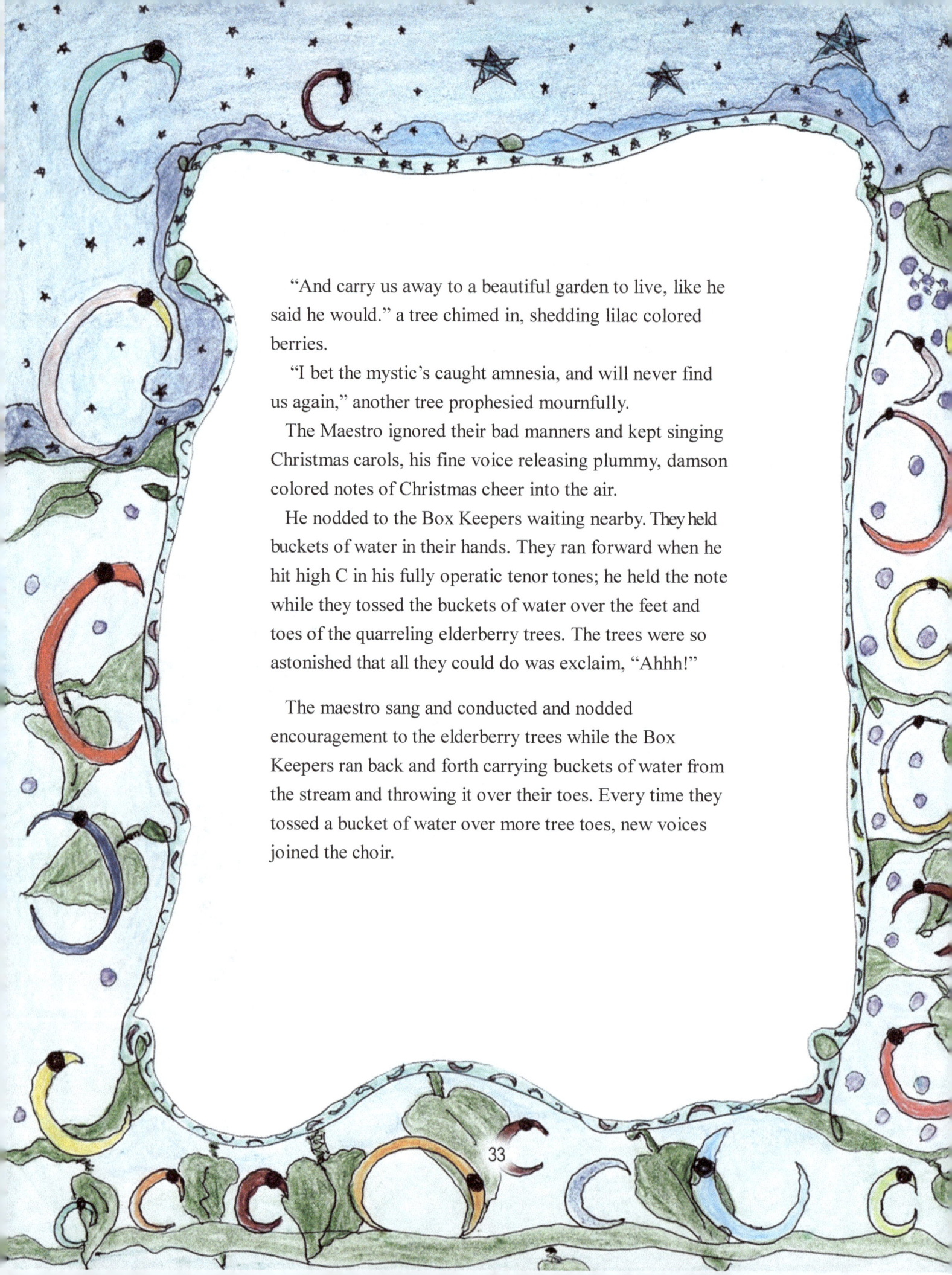

"And carry us away to a beautiful garden to live, like he said he would." a tree chimed in, shedding lilac colored berries.

"I bet the mystic's caught amnesia, and will never find us again," another tree prophesied mournfully.

The Maestro ignored their bad manners and kept singing Christmas carols, his fine voice releasing plummy, damson colored notes of Christmas cheer into the air.

He nodded to the Box Keepers waiting nearby. They held buckets of water in their hands. They ran forward when he hit high C in his fully operatic tenor tones; he held the note while they tossed the buckets of water over the feet and toes of the quarreling elderberry trees. The trees were so astonished that all they could do was exclaim, "Ahhh!"

The maestro sang and conducted and nodded encouragement to the elderberry trees while the Box Keepers ran back and forth carrying buckets of water from the stream and throwing it over their toes. Every time they tossed a bucket of water over more tree toes, new voices joined the choir.

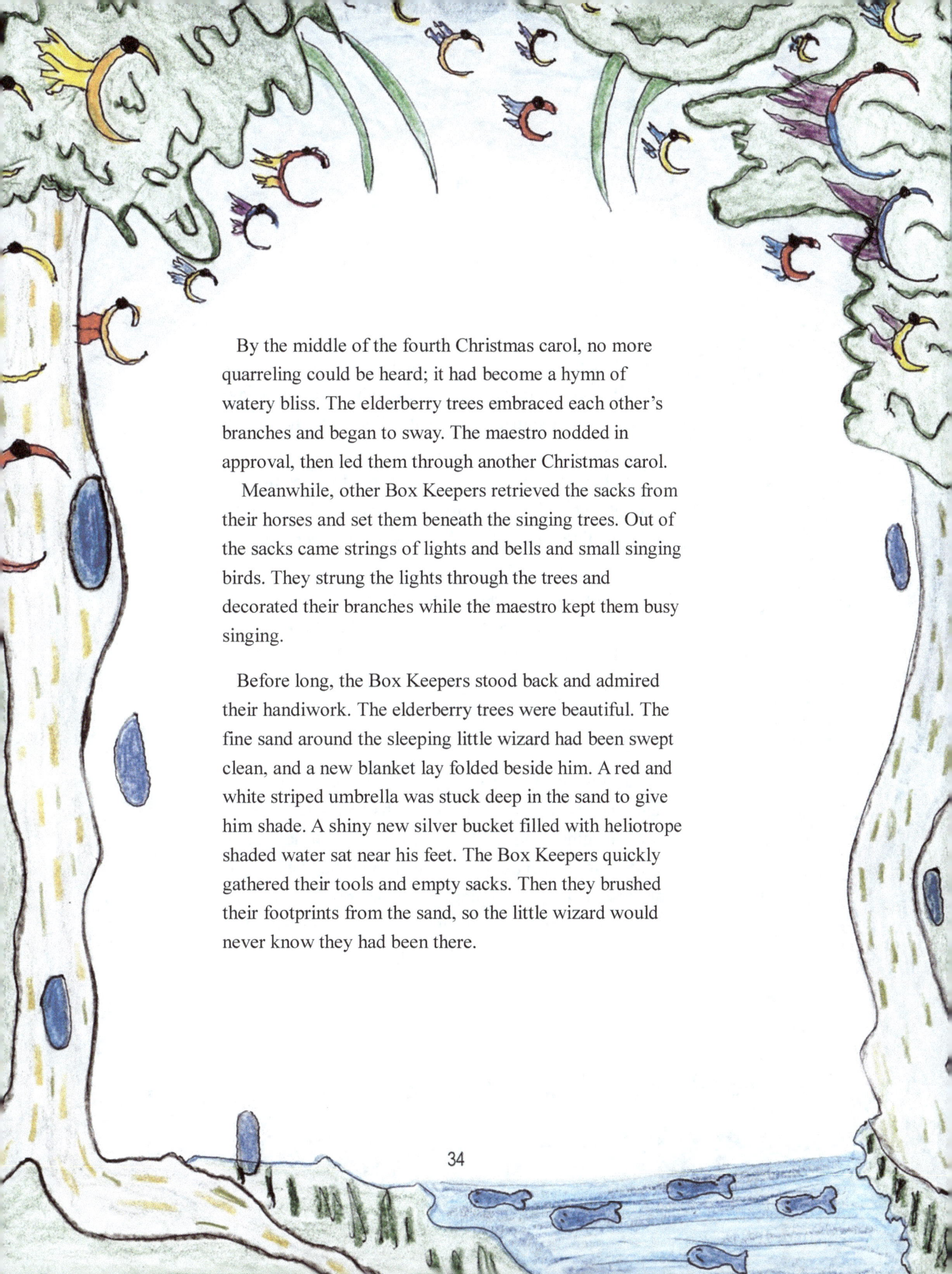

By the middle of the fourth Christmas carol, no more quarreling could be heard; it had become a hymn of watery bliss. The elderberry trees embraced each other's branches and began to sway. The maestro nodded in approval, then led them through another Christmas carol.

Meanwhile, other Box Keepers retrieved the sacks from their horses and set them beneath the singing trees. Out of the sacks came strings of lights and bells and small singing birds. They strung the lights through the trees and decorated their branches while the maestro kept them busy singing.

Before long, the Box Keepers stood back and admired their handiwork. The elderberry trees were beautiful. The fine sand around the sleeping little wizard had been swept clean, and a new blanket lay folded beside him. A red and white striped umbrella was stuck deep in the sand to give him shade. A shiny new silver bucket filled with heliotrope shaded water sat near his feet. The Box Keepers quickly gathered their tools and empty sacks. Then they brushed their footprints from the sand, so the little wizard would never know they had been there.

With that, the Box Keepers who had hummed in the little wizard's ears tiptoed to their horses. They all rode away, satisfied with the magic they had delivered to the almost forgotten, little, lost desert oasis.

For after all, everyone everywhere has to wend their way through this world, and learn what they need to know and do, but a little magic goes a long way towards good, especially at Christmas.

The little wizard woke up. He yawned mightily and glanced up at the cheerful umbrella shading him. In a flash, he was on his feet, standing far away from it. He crept closer and closer, and bumped into the bucket. It tipped over and water spilled across his toes.
In surprise, he exclaimed, "Ahhh!"

Immediately, the elderberry trees, who had been humming as they contemplated each other's new finery, began singing another Christmas carol. The little wizard looked around, amazed at all the changes that had taken place while he was napping. He rubbed his eyes and tapped his sharp little chin and muttered to himself, "I must have slept longer than I thought!"

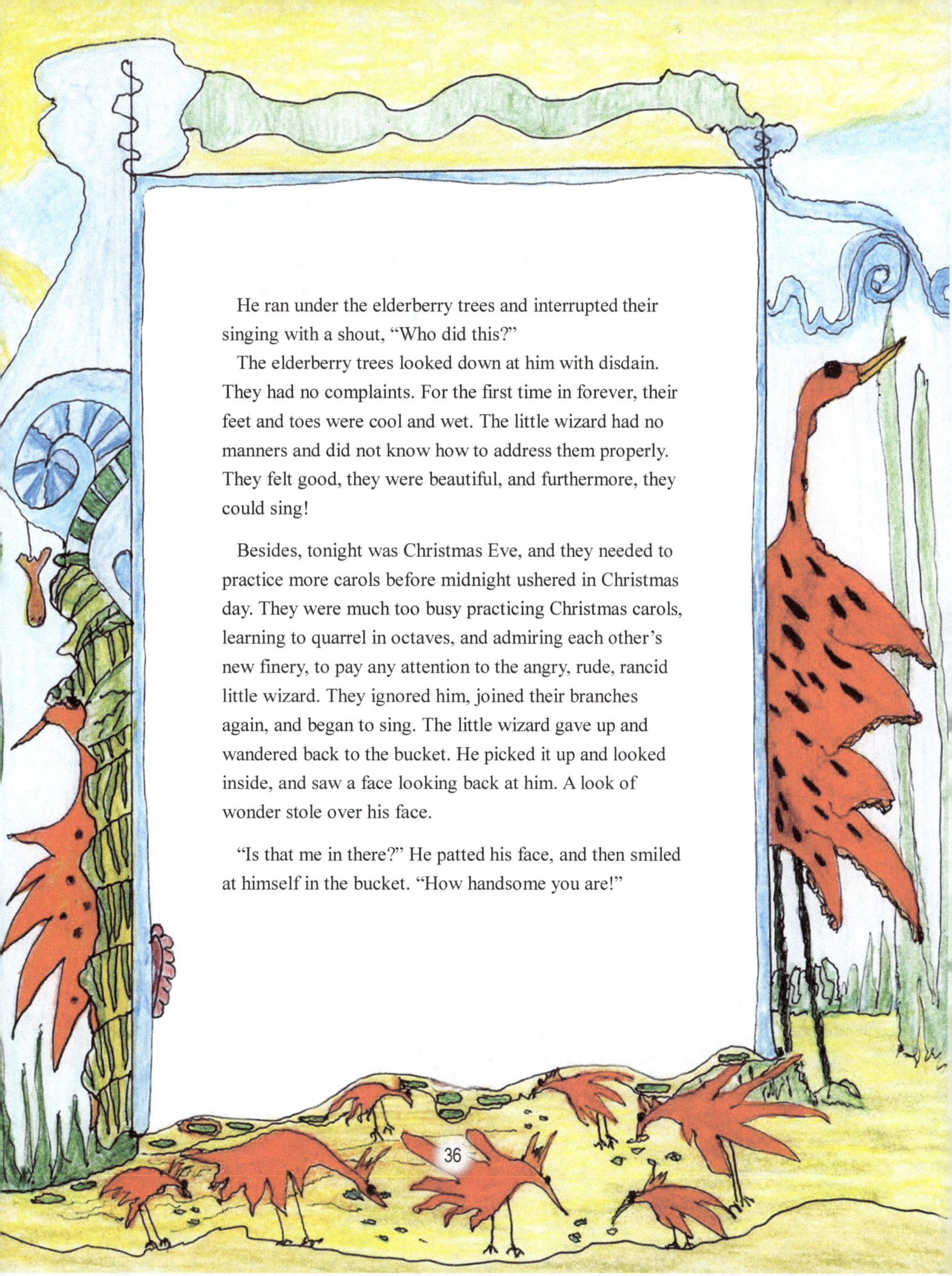

He ran under the elderberry trees and interrupted their singing with a shout, "Who did this?"

The elderberry trees looked down at him with disdain. They had no complaints. For the first time in forever, their feet and toes were cool and wet. The little wizard had no manners and did not know how to address them properly. They felt good, they were beautiful, and furthermore, they could sing!

Besides, tonight was Christmas Eve, and they needed to practice more carols before midnight ushered in Christmas day. They were much too busy practicing Christmas carols, learning to quarrel in octaves, and admiring each other's new finery, to pay any attention to the angry, rude, rancid little wizard. They ignored him, joined their branches again, and began to sing. The little wizard gave up and wandered back to the bucket. He picked it up and looked inside, and saw a face looking back at him. A look of wonder stole over his face.

"Is that me in there?" He patted his face, and then smiled at himself in the bucket. "How handsome you are!"

For a while, he groomed his hair back from his face with his fingers and practiced smiling at the handsome image in the bucket. Suddenly he stopped and a crafty look stole over his face. He gave the pottering, puttering, dabbling little purple stream a sneaky glance, and tiptoed over to the water. The little purple stream paid no attention to him. It was too busy smoothing the new sand in its stream bed, and at the same time, being cooled by the small stones and listening to their stories.

The small and still smelly little wizard dipped the bucket in the stream. Instantly it filled to the brim with mauve and lavender water. He lifted the bucket high and poured the cool water over his head. He shouted, "Ahhh!"

He dropped the bucket and threw himself into the wisteria and Tuscan magenta water flowing at his feet. He shouted again, "Aahhh!" After all, it had been even more weeks and weeks of concentrated reeks before any water had become available.

The elderberry trees heard him and promptly broke into another Christmas carol. After splashing about in the violet and dark purple water for a long time, the little wizard was no longer rancid, stinky, or even smelly. He was a perfectly clean little wizard, with just a hint of deep orchid to his skin.

Darkness came, and the little wizard sat on the bank of the now grape, fandango, and heliotrope colored stream to watch the stars come out. He felt very clean and mighty in his thankfulness.

Midnight drew near. He went and stood under the elderberry trees while they sang. When he began singing along with them, they did not object, even though he sang off key. In the clear, starry night, the small and now very clean little wizard lifted his hands to the sky and gave much loud singing to everything around him.
"Huzza Huzza up there!" he shouted up at the sky, waving his hands.
"Abra Cadabra!"
At last, the elderberry trees stopped singing and went to sleep with their lights glowing in the deep purple night.
"Good night," they said to each other.
The little wizard prepared for sleep and curled up in his new blanket under the red and white umbrella.

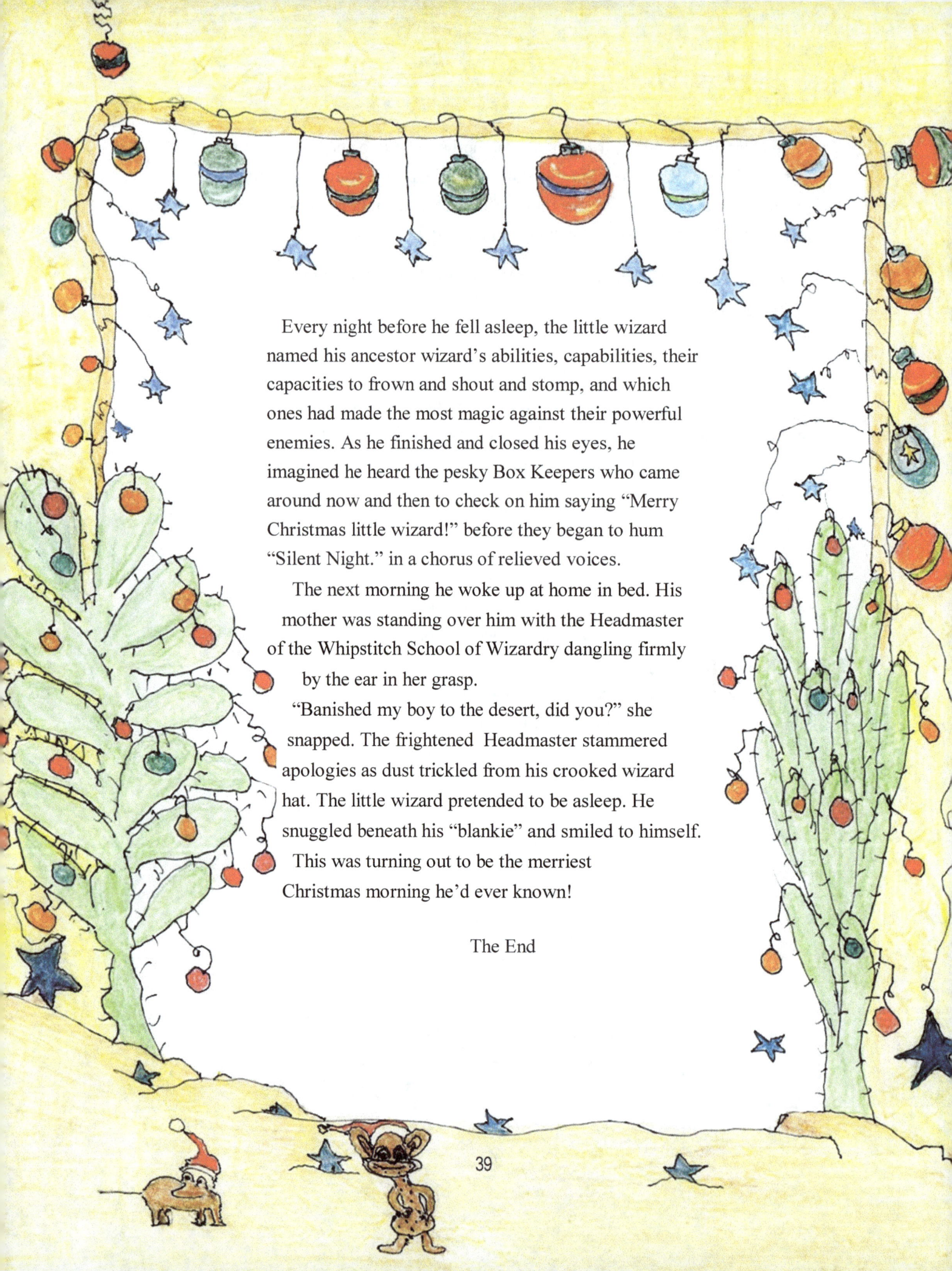

Every night before he fell asleep, the little wizard named his ancestor wizard's abilities, capabilities, their capacities to frown and shout and stomp, and which ones had made the most magic against their powerful enemies. As he finished and closed his eyes, he imagined he heard the pesky Box Keepers who came around now and then to check on him saying "Merry Christmas little wizard!" before they began to hum "Silent Night." in a chorus of relieved voices.

The next morning he woke up at home in bed. His mother was standing over him with the Headmaster of the Whipstitch School of Wizardry dangling firmly by the ear in her grasp.

"Banished my boy to the desert, did you?" she snapped. The frightened Headmaster stammered apologies as dust trickled from his crooked wizard hat. The little wizard pretended to be asleep. He snuggled beneath his "blankie" and smiled to himself. This was turning out to be the merriest Christmas morning he'd ever known!

The End

2

Sam, the Crabby Hermit Boy and the Alchemist's Box

"Alone is a place
amid the rest
where each one is singular
and each one is blessed."

Once upon a time, in the loneliest part of the Kingdom, a hermit boy lived in a hut hidden deep in a forest of wildly waving trees decorated with reds, greens and sometimes purple ornaments. The reasons the trees danced deep in the snowy, blowy forest is a story for another time. And that story must be told only when the magic of the moon encounters the lonely places in the Kingdom where old enchantments still linger…

But this particular story is about a hermit boy. This hermit boy was named Sam but he had no reason to say his name because there was no one around to say it to.

In those days of long ago, just as it still is today, hermits are people who live far away from other people, mostly because they want to.

Every hermit has their own reasons for withdrawing from the society of others, reasons they don't share because they are hermits. Sam the hermit boy was crabby and ornery and baffling, just like most hermits are.

Some things never change.

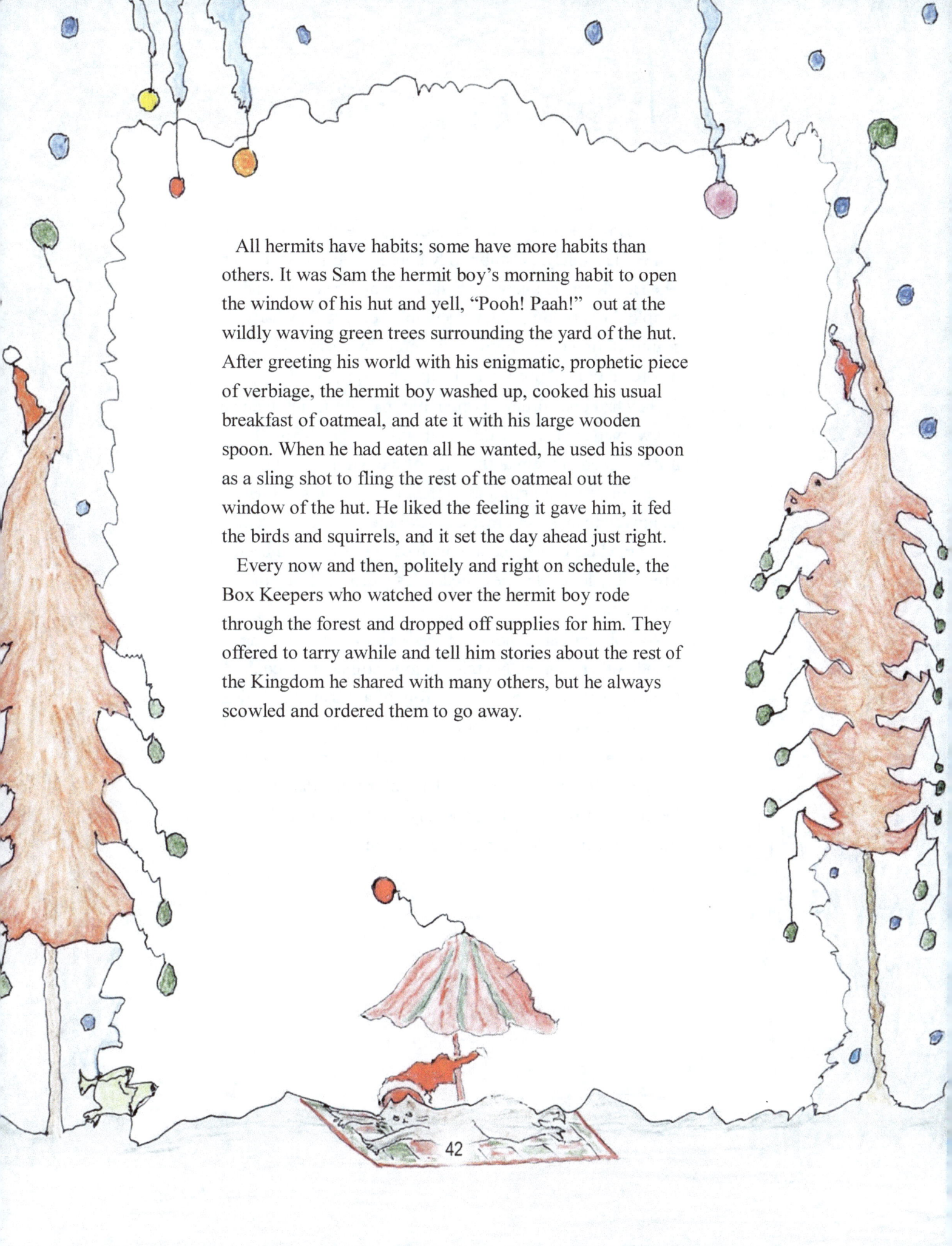

All hermits have habits; some have more habits than others. It was Sam the hermit boy's morning habit to open the window of his hut and yell, "Pooh! Paah!" out at the wildly waving green trees surrounding the yard of the hut. After greeting his world with his enigmatic, prophetic piece of verbiage, the hermit boy washed up, cooked his usual breakfast of oatmeal, and ate it with his large wooden spoon. When he had eaten all he wanted, he used his spoon as a sling shot to fling the rest of the oatmeal out the window of the hut. He liked the feeling it gave him, it fed the birds and squirrels, and it set the day ahead just right.

Every now and then, politely and right on schedule, the Box Keepers who watched over the hermit boy rode through the forest and dropped off supplies for him. They offered to tarry awhile and tell him stories about the rest of the Kingdom he shared with many others, but he always scowled and ordered them to go away.

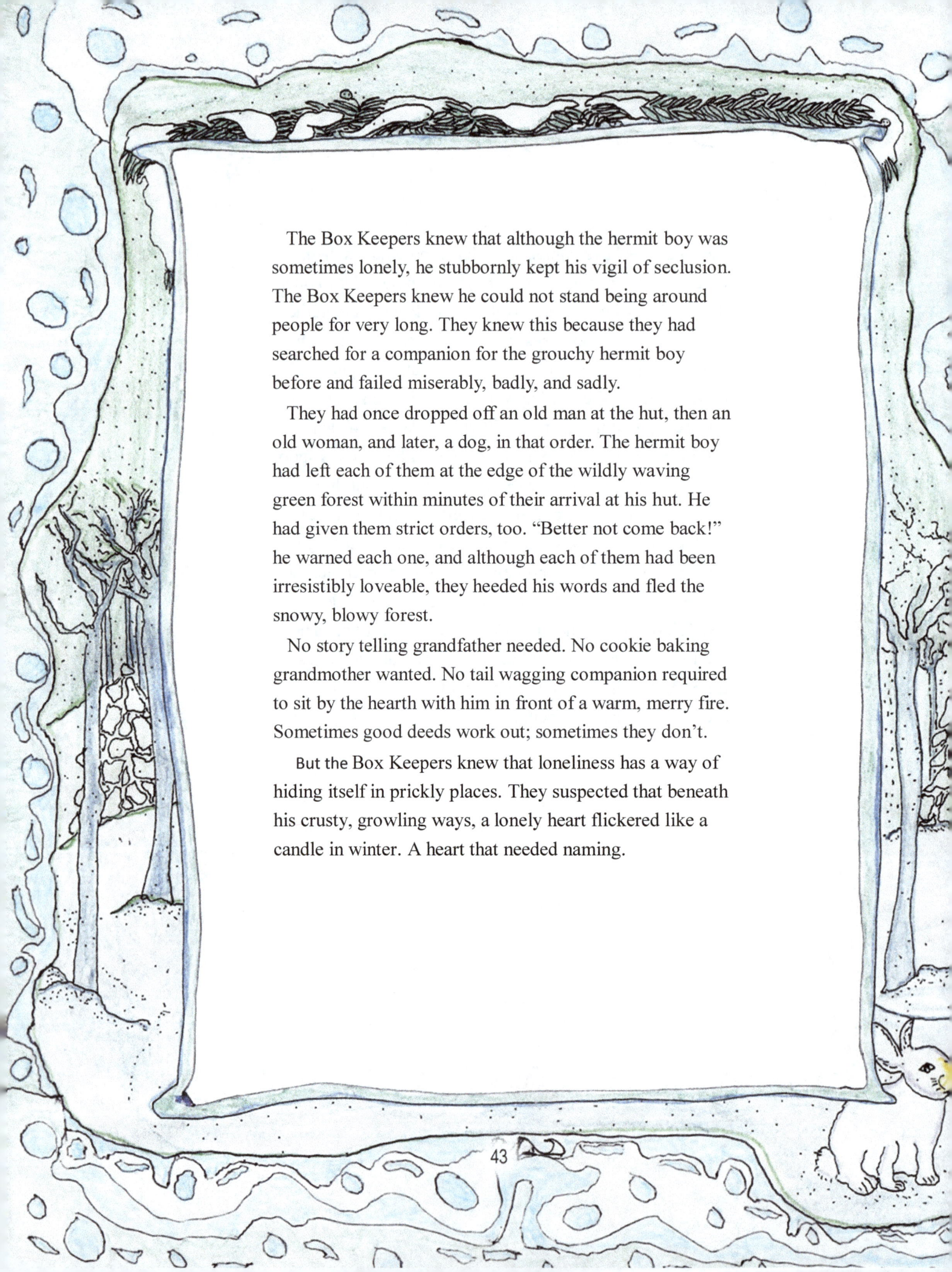

The Box Keepers knew that although the hermit boy was sometimes lonely, he stubbornly kept his vigil of seclusion. The Box Keepers knew he could not stand being around people for very long. They knew this because they had searched for a companion for the grouchy hermit boy before and failed miserably, badly, and sadly.

They had once dropped off an old man at the hut, then an old woman, and later, a dog, in that order. The hermit boy had left each of them at the edge of the wildly waving green forest within minutes of their arrival at his hut. He had given them strict orders, too. "Better not come back!" he warned each one, and although each of them had been irresistibly loveable, they heeded his words and fled the snowy, blowy forest.

No story telling grandfather needed. No cookie baking grandmother wanted. No tail wagging companion required to sit by the hearth with him in front of a warm, merry fire. Sometimes good deeds work out; sometimes they don't.

But the Box Keepers knew that loneliness has a way of hiding itself in prickly places. They suspected that beneath his crusty, growling ways, a lonely heart flickered like a candle in winter. A heart that needed naming.

Time passed, and Christmas drew near. The Box Keepers
decided to try one last time to find a special Christmas
gift for the hermit boy. But try as they might, they
couldn't think of anything surly, yet entertaining
enough for him. They decided to visit the Crones' castle and
ask for help. They did not want to fail again. The Crones and
the Box Keepers searched the kingdom over for just the right
gift for the hermit boy, but they found nothing.

They decided to ask the oldest Crone in the Crone's
castle for her advice.

Now, everyone dwelling in the magic
Kingdom inside the old abandoned shoe box factory is
assigned a magic name depending on the habits
and powers each one has acquired. Often, many
names are tried on before one that fits just right
sticks.

Elder Silverado Foggy Fitz was the oldest
Crone in the Kingdom. The wisdom she
had accrued through her many ages had
made her very tall and prone to wearing
hats that wobbled mysteriously when she
was thinking.

Her wisdom emanated like a smudgy, hazy halo around her head. As far back as anyone could remember, she had been an installation in the Crones' castle; that meant she was a permanent, artistic specialist in things not known to others. A lot of Elders specialize in that particular field. The Crones and everyone else in the castle secretly called her "Foggy Fitz" for short.

Now, it just so happened that Elder Silverado Foggy Fitz knew two things the rest of them didn't. One, she had been beloved by an old alchemist for a short time; and two, she knew that all hermits were alchemists in training.

When the Box Keepers and Crones asked for help, she said, "Ah!" and sank into a thoughtful silence.

Her questioners had expected as much. They conked off to sleep, believing the answer might take a while. She searched her mind until she remembered the chamber where the white haired, absent minded old alchemist who had loved her many years ago had lived. He had lived for a short and fairly explosive time deep in a secret room in the castle.

All that had been left behind was his old alchemist's box. Rising, she bid the Box Keepers, Crones and Others to awaken. After a long search through labyrinths and dusty tunnels, she discovered the old alchemist's box sitting on a shelf in a dark corner of an abandoned room.

The old alchemist's box had, of course, a silver star on its lid, which denoted that it was an alchemist's box, and definitely not a shoe box, nor a lunch box, nor a hat box, nor any other kind of box.

Dense, dark clouds rumbled and grumbled and bumped into each other above the ancient alchemist's box. Every now and then, a train whistle or the sound of hammering came from inside the box. It glowered at the world, lifting its lid quite often to let out groans and moans, complaints, and unusual smells that were not altogether polite. Cheese grating was not a mystery to the old alchemist's box. In fact, it was very good at cheese grating, particularly Limburger and Munster.

The old alchemist's box had sat on the shelf alone and forgotten for many yearrs. Over time it had become mysterious, intense, forlorn and forsaken, and smelly, as many lonely old things do. Its silver star dimmed and its pride and crankiness prevented the old box from saying how rejected and desolate it felt. It believed no one wanted old things.

46

Now, many old things bear an intensity accumulated from the inevitable accrual of unused, unwanted wisdom, and a polite yet persistent need to polish silverware by moonlight. Such was Elder Silverado Foggy Fitz . She lifted the alchemist's box from the shelf and wiped the cobwebs and dust from the old alchemist's box. She held it a long while, memories flowing of the lost love that had disappeared in an explosion leaving only soot, boots, and the alchemist's box behind. Finally, she held the box out to the Box Keepers. They looked it over. It was frowning and emitting cheesy smells, frugal threats and hissing. They knew right away the box was destined to be the hermit boy's perfect Christmas gift.

They rubbed their hands together in delight and grinned at each other, exclaiming, "At last!" It was time for the old alchemist's box to be passed on.

The day before Christmas, the Box Keepers dressed in their finery and made their way to the hermit boy's hut. The forest trees flung ornaments at them and waved as they rode through the forest.

The hermit boy heard them and looked out the window. He had just finished his oatmeal, with a gooey and goodly amount left to spare. He scowled at the visitors, opened the window, and flung a large spoonful of oatmeal out the window at them.

"Pooh! Paah! Go away!" he shouted.

He slammed the window shut. The Box Keepers carried his gifts through the swirling snow to the middle of the yard.

With an abundance of pomp and ceremony, they unfurled a new cloak, spread it on the ground and stacked the rest of the Christmas presents on it. Then, with several "Hear ye's!" and without further ado, they marched to the door of the hut and hung a hero's medal around the knob, then settled the alchemist's box into the snow beside the steps. That done, they marched to the center of the yard, drew out trumpets and blew warning blasts on them, for it is always best to blow a warning fanfare before giving anyone an alchemist's box. Then they rode swiftly away. The hermit boy listened to their hurried retreat before he opened the window and stared out at the gifts stacked on the new cloak. He heard a loud groan.

"Who's there? I am the only one allowed on this place!" the hermit boy shouted. The alchemist's box was wide awake. It realized it was sitting outside in swirling snow that threatened to cover it any minute. Its life would soon be over. It groaned in abject misery. Why had the cruel Box Keepers carried it all this way? Just to abandon it, to leave it alone and unseen in the snow by this dilapidated little dwelling? It lifted its lid and chuffed out a loud hiccup of sorrow.

The hermit boy opened the door. The hero's medal banged against it. He carried the hero's medal into the hut and laid it on the table, then went back outside to gather the gifts and the cloak. Back and forth he went, spreading the cloak across a chair to dry, carrying the gifts inside.

He never noticed the snow-covered alchemist's box sitting beside the front steps. He made his last trip, went back inside and closed the door. The snow kept falling, layering itself over the old alchemist's box. The box shivered in its place by the steps, lifting its lid slightly from time to time to let out complaints.

It knew all was lost, and its life would probably end by the steps, buried under a blanket of snow. It realized its long, previously useful existence in the military and later, companion to the lovelorn wandering alchemist would soon be meaningless and forgotten.

It tried to lift its lid again but the weight of the snow was holding it shut. The box was frightened. A mighty Groan and an expanding smell began gathering strength inside it. The heavy, dark clouds hanging over the box grew darker and darker. They rumbled and grumbled and thumped into each other, throwing off sizzling lightning flashes that singed the snow around the box. The Groan grew bigger and louder inside the box until at last, the lid burst open.

Out flew the Groan. It roared, "Help!" as it flew across the yard and landed on its back in the snow. The surly hermit boy, snugly wrapped in his new cloak, was napping by the fireplace when the Groan's roar for help woke him up. He jumped up and ran out the door just in time to watch the Groan roll to a stop in the snow. The snow slid off the alchemist's box and it stayed open. The old box had plenty to say about what it had been through.

It huffed and fumed and grumbled and rumbled. "Think you not that you can best me, you bedraggled bunch of villainous Box Keepers that left me sitting out in the snow and wind! I shall not perish without a fight!"

The box gathered more air and ire and continued, "How dare you abandon me out in this snow to perish beside this crude, tasteless, unadorned little hut, with no erstwhile companion to suffer with me? I am an alchemist's magic box, and as such, will not put up with this!"

The dark rumbling clouds above the alchemist's box banged into each other and sent out lightning bolts that sizzled when they hit the snow around the box. The mighty Groan, covered in snow, staggered back over to the box and sat down beside it. "Help!" the mighty Groan roared again, interrupting the box's oratory narrative of indignation.

The box stopped grumbling for a moment, and a mysterious smell poured out of it, causing the mighty Groan to flee across the yard once again to its farthest reaches.

It fell on its back and lay speechless, staring up at the sky, no longer caring that all of itself was cold and wet, just thankfully unmoved by the cheesy al dente pecorino odors that had poured from the box.

The hermit boy glared down at the alchemist's box and hissed. A larger hiss answered him from the box.

"Be quiet!" he ordered. His sleep had been interrupted, and insurrection was not allowed in his yard!

The box hissed back at him.

The hermit boy said, "I've had enough of you!"

He ran down the steps and grabbed the alchemist's box. It let out a surprised yelp.

"Nobody manhandles me, you silly boy!"

Bolts of lightning flew out of the dark, rumbling clouds hovering over the box. They struck the hermit boy's hands, jolted up his arms, and kept zipping upward until his hair stood at attention and his eyes opened wider than they ever would or could again.

Weaving back and forth in the snow, he remembered the warning fanfare the Box Keepers had played just before they skedaddled. He shook his head to clear it and yelled at the alchemist's box.

"They were warning me about YOU, weren't they?"

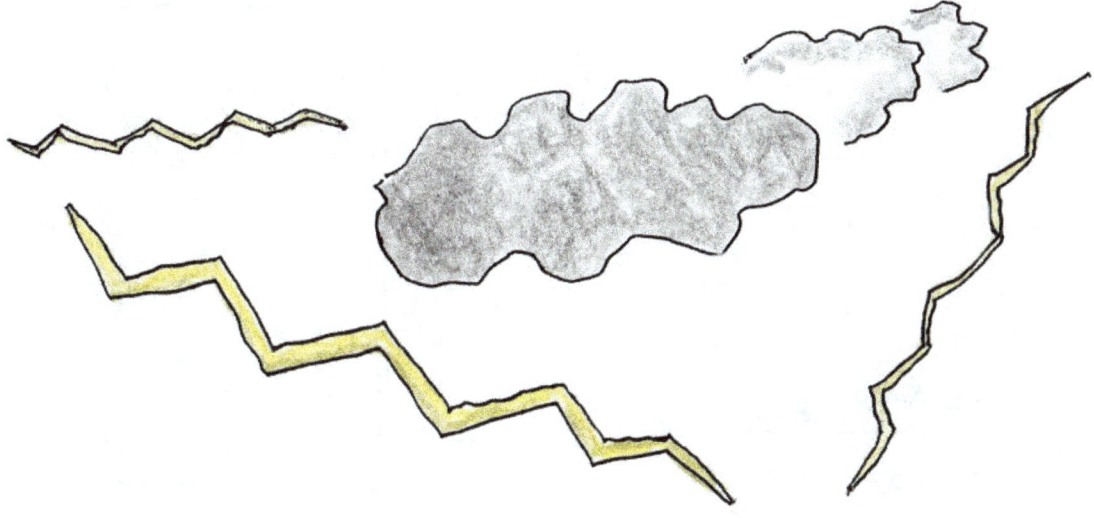

He shut the lid of the box and rushed up the steps with it. He placed the box on the table. The box's lid flew open again, and it continued complaining. The dark clouds above it rumbled and threw off lightning bolts while the hermit boy wisely maintained a goodly distance.

"See, I am not done in because of this horrible weather. It is unquestionably evident that I have been mishandled by those vagrant Box Keepers!"

The alchemist's box continued its tirade of complaints. It listed its heartbreak, rejections, aches and pains. It went on and on. And on and on. And on. The ornery hermit boy pulled up a chair and listened as it sorted through its complaints. His edgy, hurt heart began to thaw. After a while, though he tended towards maintaining a sterile and mostly ominous atmosphere, he found himself admiring the complaining style compiled and communicated by the grumpy, elderly alchemist's box. It was an impressive achievement, an utter alchemy of adjectives, adverbs and all things grammatical.

Little by little, the crabby hermit boy joined in. The old alchemist's box answered him, complaint for complaint. The night passed swiftly while they became acquainted. Morning dawned, bright and clear. The hermit boy cooked his oatmeal and when it was ready, he ladled out a heaping spoonful. He lifted the lid of the box and flung the oatmeal inside. The old alchemist's box said in surprise, "Hmm?"

It closed its lid. After a moment, it lifted it again to let out a small, discreet burp. The hermit boy answered with a burp of his own. Then he picked up the hero's medal, lifted the lid of the box, and dropped it in.

"Here's your Christmas present." he said in a gruff voice. A surprised rumble came from the box. Then it lifted its lid, and said in a surly voice, "I know a lonesome hero's story if you would like to hear it sometime."

"Well, can the Hero be named Sam? That's my name."

He placed a finger to his lips.

"But don't ever tell anyone. What is your name?"

"Well, they called me Hedge back in my military days. You know, for being a bit prickly?"

Sam the hermit boy looked at the box and nodded. "Hedge, it is."

Then they both roared "Pooh! and Paah," just to let off steam. The box began a military chant in a voice that reminded the hermit boy of a rusty, squeaky old door hinge. When he finished, the box sighed and looked up woefully at Sam and whispered, "A terrible loneliness has informed my life for many a day, Sam."

Sam nodded. "Hedge, you definitely are a ham," He picked up the ladle and tapped the box on both sides of its silver star. The star began to shine. "Never more," he said to the alchemist's box. "Never more."

Then he went to the window, opened it and the two of them shouted, "Pooh" and "Paah," while he flung the rest of the oatmeal out the window.

Before long the sounds of loud, rusty singing and the enumerating of alchemy equivalents poured through the forest while the waving green trees tossed ornaments at each other, and the snow counted its cornices and circumferences in tempo with the alchemy equivalents.

A new place had been created, a new address for two who weren't alone any more.
Sam and Hedge.

The End

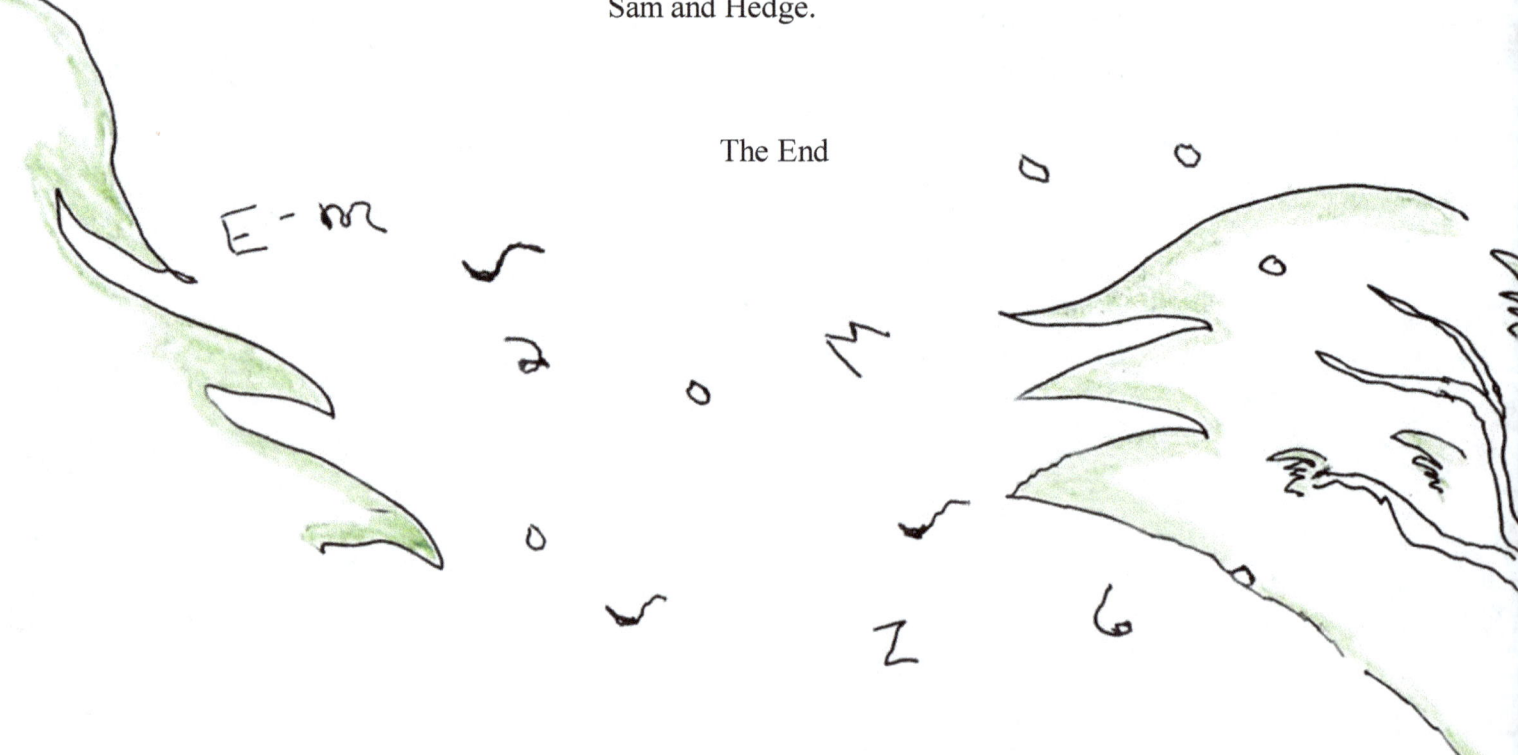

3 The Tolling Midnight Bells
that Chimed Christmas

From "Reflections"

"Peace reigns best,
When night is blest."

A gorgeous blue magic box trimmed with ornate golden edges, a box just the right size to hold a small child's dancing slippers, sat on a shelf in an ancient stone church in a far off land. Dust was layered thick and heavy over the box. Sometimes, the music in the ancient church curled its curious edges around the beautiful blue and gold magic box and asked questions and stayed there awhile. But the magic box never answered, and the music moved away.

Inside the magic box lay a little spirit, fast asleep. The little spirit had been sleeping for a long time. The smell of incense, the sound of bells tolling and music playing, and the many strange languages strolling by the dusty box did not disturb its slumber. Sometimes it stirred and stretched and sighed, turned over, and almost woke up. It was tiny footprints and fairy dust waiting to be born.

Far away in a distant land, on the edge of a big city filled with night lights, as far away from the old church as dreams could be, stood a tall, thin house, number 11, squeezed close by other tall, thin houses.

Number 11 was pitch dark like all the thin houses huddled up against it, except for one dim light shining in an upstairs window. The light came from a lamp on a tiny table beside the bed of a sleeping child.

A Box Keeper knelt by the bed and took the sleeping child's hand in his. The child woke up and smiled at him. The Box Keeper took the measure of the dark blue of the midnight sky beginning to gather in the child's eyes before the child closed its eyes again.

He held the little hand tenderly until the child slept before he left the cold, dank little bedroom and trod down the dark, twisting stair steps. Out on the dimly lit street, he studied the tiny light glowing in the window above him for a long time before he strode away. He would find it. He would let nothing stop him. He began to search for it everywhere.

Time passed. A letter arrived at the old church in the far-off land. Footsteps came towards the blue magic box trimmed with gold edges. The little spirit in the box stirred in its sleep. Footsteps came closer, hands touched the box, picked it up, and carried it away.

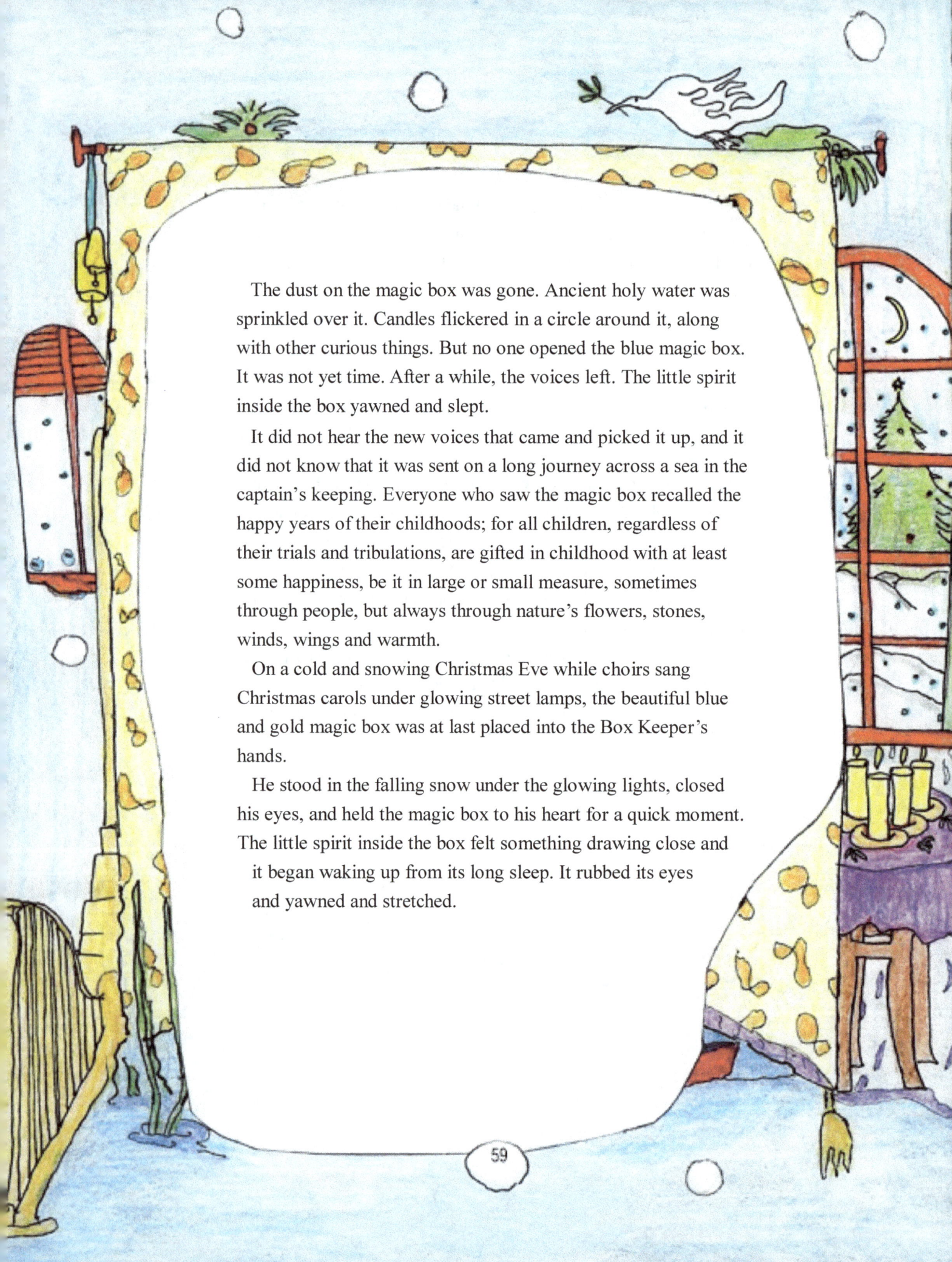

The dust on the magic box was gone. Ancient holy water was sprinkled over it. Candles flickered in a circle around it, along with other curious things. But no one opened the blue magic box. It was not yet time. After a while, the voices left. The little spirit inside the box yawned and slept.

It did not hear the new voices that came and picked it up, and it did not know that it was sent on a long journey across a sea in the captain's keeping. Everyone who saw the magic box recalled the happy years of their childhoods; for all children, regardless of their trials and tribulations, are gifted in childhood with at least some happiness, be it in large or small measure, sometimes through people, but always through nature's flowers, stones, winds, wings and warmth.

On a cold and snowing Christmas Eve while choirs sang Christmas carols under glowing street lamps, the beautiful blue and gold magic box was at last placed into the Box Keeper's hands.

He stood in the falling snow under the glowing lights, closed his eyes, and held the magic box to his heart for a quick moment. The little spirit inside the box felt something drawing close and it began waking up from its long sleep. It rubbed its eyes and yawned and stretched.

The Box Keeper hurried through the streets until he reached Number 11. He stopped and looked up; the same dim light shone in the skinny window high above him. Quickly, he ran up the icy steps, up and up the dark, steep stairs, carefully holding the magic box close.

He hurried into the bedroom where the child lay sleeping and knelt beside the bed. He touched the child's hand. The child sat up and gathered a ragged blanket close to ward off the chill of the dank room. The Box Keeper placed the beautiful blue and gold box into the child's hands.

The lid flew open. The little spirit inside began to sing and race around in circles. It flew out and began to dance on the child's fingertips. Tiny laughs, giggles, and other sweet sounds poured out of the magic box.

A slow, sweet smile spread over the child's solemn face as the magic of fairy dust and tiny footprints made their way into the child's heart and settled there forever.

The Box Keeper's smile beamed like a beacon, and suddenly the child's tiny, dimly lit room filled with warmth and the soft scents of ginger and candy canes. He reached into the magic box and took out a pair of blue and gold dancing slippers and quickly slipped them onto the child's feet. They fit just right.

The bells of a nearby church chimed midnight, ushering in Christmas Day. The Box Keeper swept off his hat and bowed his head as more church bells rang while carolers sang of love and hope and of promises kept. Suddenly, all the old and young stopped what they were doing and listened to the pure, sweet sound of a small child's laughter drifting up to the midnight sky.

The child's laughter filled the hearts of Christmas angels, who lifted their voices in gratitude; they became shooting stars flying through the midnight sky.

4 The Rose Paper Magic Box with Warm, Red Courage

Excerpt from "One Thing More,"

"A rose picked too soon loses its bloom,
while another takes its place,
'Tis both that leave
a lasting fragrance in the air…"

In a field on a high ridge in a forgotten corner in the Kingdom of True Believers in Imagination stood a tall, empty house with many long, thin windows. The windows stared silently out over fields of wild berries and brambles surrounding the house. Past the fields and far away in the distance, was the beginning of a Great Forest.

The scarred, chipped wood of the abandoned house had weathered from white to gray. The well-traveled path that once wound its way to the front porch lay hidden beneath wild, thick runners, brambles and weeds.

Inside the house, in an upstairs bedroom, a faded rose-covered keepsake box lay on its side in the middle of the floor with its lid open. Dust motes drifted through the dim afternoon light coming through the dusty bedroom windows. Once, long ago, the box was treasured by a happy young girl with dreams.

Everyone living nearby avoided the abandoned house. Yet now and then, someone claimed to see a soft light glowing in the upstairs bedroom where the rose paper box lay open beside the bed of the missing girl who never truly left the house behind.

The tattered lace curtains fluttered and whispered of days of long ago when
they were new and treasured by the lovely young maiden who slept and dreamed
in the bedroom. The bedroom listened. The floorboards creaked. The roses outside
brushed against the porch roof.

   Somewhere deep within the old house, time itself sighed, remembering
laughter, candlelight, and the sweet sounds of a girl's voice. The rose paper
magic box lay on the floor, waiting for the maiden's return.
Sometimes, when the moonlight poured through the windows late at
night, the curtains heard the patter of rain and smelt
the scent of good earth coming
from inside the box.

   The only visitors the house had were the Moon and the Sun and
Spring, Summer, Fall, and Winter. The curious Moon liked the
lonesome old house sitting atop a ridge, surrounded by fields of wild things.
The Moon came and went, peeking through the windows of the old house.
   When the Moon was full, it poured its strongest light through the maiden's
bedroom window, causing the ragged lace curtains to rustle back and forth
and the rose paper magic box to pour out plaintive love songs.

As much as the Moon loved visiting the old house, Winter loved visiting the old house most of all. Each year, Winter filled each crack and crevice of the old house with snow and ice. As the years passed, Winter stayed there longer and longer, until finally, it never left.

Ice and snow blanketed the porch and windows. The birds left their nests in the eaves and trees and flew away to warmer places. The flowers and berries that grew in the fields froze and turned brown and brittle with ice. No animals dared cross the frozen fields around the old house. The seasons came and went everywhere else in the Kingdom, but the lonely, old, dozing house, standing tall atop its ridge, stayed frozen in the powerful grip of Winter.

The Crones who visited with the Moon knew about the part of Winter that had moved into the old house. They knew about the rose paper magic box and the magic and memories living on inside it.

The seasons changed, and Winter came once again, settling itself over the Kingdom. Christmas drew near. The Crones were busy with their Yuletide preparations. One night, the Moon visited the Crones and told them the old house was in danger of freezing and tumbling apart if Winter tarried there much longer. The Crones nodded to each other. It was time to send a Box Keeper out to the old house.

The day before Christmas, a Crone went into a ritual room, selected a Silver Web from a shelf and carried it away. The Silver Web trembled and gleamed with excitement as the Crone wrapped it in a small, warm shawl and gently handed it to a Box Keeper, one who knew how to ice skate, fashion ice sculptures and knew the meaning of ice cubes; he was a Box Keeper who bore a great and lasting admiration for winter and its many foibles. The Box Keeper placed the Silver Web in his magic box and left for the old rose house.

Snow crunched loudly under the hooves of his horse as the Box Keeper rode across the frozen yard of the old house. He studied the ice covered fields surrounding the old house, the snowdrifts deckling the faded, lonesome corners of fence and house. Frozen red roses had twined themselves around the porch posts and hanging from the roof. The windows were thick with frost patterns keeping the sunlight out and the cold in. Winter had its own wisdom about how things should be done.

The porch steps were thick with sleet. The Box Keeper, well versed in the ways of Winter, nodded to himself and thought, "Winter has certainly remained here a long time."

He dismounted, carefully made his way up the porch steps and across the frozen porch to the front door. He pushed, and it creaked and groaned loudly as it swung open. The thin, ragged curtains hanging over the maiden's bedroom windows rustled in excitement when they heard the door open. They listened as footsteps echoed through the empty house, then found their way up the stairs to the maiden's bedroom door. They trembled and watched as the knob turned and the bedroom door creaked open.

The Box Keeper stood in the doorway and peered into the vacant, dusty room. He looked at the ragged, dancing, hopeful curtains, and the dusty rose paper magic box laying on the floor on its side with its lid open.

He doffed his hat and bowed to the curtains before he crossed to the rose paper magic box and knelt beside it. He took a large, bright white handkerchief from his pocket and gently wiped the dust off the box. Then he put the handkerchief back into his pocket, closed the lid of the box and picked it up. He turned and left the room, closing the door behind him. The thin, tattered curtains sighed as they listened to the sound of his retreating footsteps and the front door opening and closing.

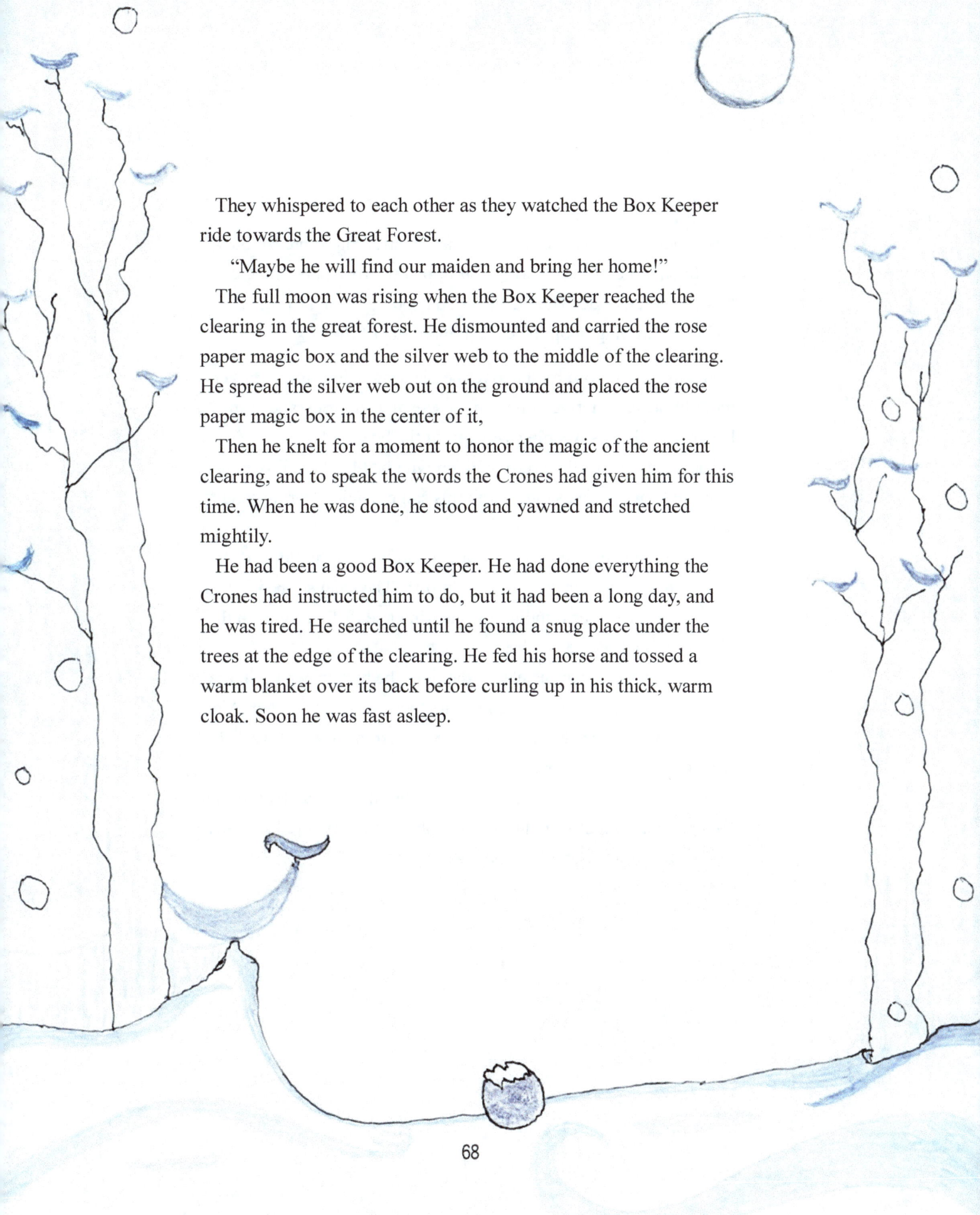

They whispered to each other as they watched the Box Keeper ride towards the Great Forest.

"Maybe he will find our maiden and bring her home!"

The full moon was rising when the Box Keeper reached the clearing in the great forest. He dismounted and carried the rose paper magic box and the silver web to the middle of the clearing. He spread the silver web out on the ground and placed the rose paper magic box in the center of it,

Then he knelt for a moment to honor the magic of the ancient clearing, and to speak the words the Crones had given him for this time. When he was done, he stood and yawned and stretched mightily.

He had been a good Box Keeper. He had done everything the Crones had instructed him to do, but it had been a long day, and he was tired. He searched until he found a snug place under the trees at the edge of the clearing. He fed his horse and tossed a warm blanket over its back before curling up in his thick, warm cloak. Soon he was fast asleep.

No sooner had his eyes closed, than an errant little breeze blew into the middle of the clearing and tipped the rose paper magic box over on its side. The lid flew open and the sound of thunder and rain pattering upon the earth poured out of the box.

The full moon rose high above the clearing, bathing it in silver moonlight. A plaintive song composed of memories and hopes began wending its weeping way out of the box.

The song was for the pretty maiden who had held the box in her arms and danced and sang to it in this same magic clearing long ago.

The box remembered all the years it had lain on the floor of the bedroom, waiting for the maiden's return. The song sobbed its way through the trees surrounding the clearing and drifted through the air and into a little nearby hut.

A young woman was asleep in the hut. She had grown up in the Great Forest, spending her early years there with her mother. Alone now, she kept to herself, avoiding the rare stranger who traveled through the Great Forest.

The mournful little song crept into the hut through a crack round the door, causing the young girl to dream of the dried red rose her mother had given her when she was a small child.

The rose had come from her mother's childhood home. Just as the mournful little song floated back out through the crack of the door, the girl awoke and jumped out of bed. Quickly she pulled on her slippers, wrapped a rose-colored cloak around herself, and followed the song back to the clearing. At the edge of the clearing, she stopped and gazed in wonder at the rose paper magic box laying on the silver web in the middle of the clearing. The song she had followed was coming from the box.

Upon hearing the faint tune and the even fainter footsteps of the young woman, the Box Keeper awoke. He looked up. The Moon stood high overhead, bathing the clearing in moon light.

He sat up and looked around. Large snowflakes drifted steadily to the ground. Tiny bells chimed softly from their places in the snow-covered tree branches above him. Lights glowed in the trees and all around the magic clearing. Fragrant bundles of herbs and grasses lay here and there. Birds flew in and out of the trees, singing and nibbling seeds and nuts.

Deer and rabbit, and every other kind of animal living in the Great Forest were gathered in the clearing, eating grains and other foods. All the four-leggeds and winged animals circled and flitted around the clearing without any fear of each other. Indeed, their hearts were filled with peace.

Through the falling snow, the Box Keeper watched the beautiful young woman dancing in the middle of the clearing. The silver web floated and gleamed around her shoulders as she cradled the rose paper magic box in her arms.

A glow came from the box, and the Box Keeper smelled the sweet scent of the red rose petals falling from the box, sprinkling the snow around her feet with warm, red courage. He watched as the girl took a paper out of the box and read it. Suddenly, he fell asleep again.

The next morning, the Box Keeper awoke. He strolled to the center of the empty clearing and took the snow white handkerchief holding the rose paper dust in it out of his pocket. He shook the handkerchief and the ancient dust in it whirled away in the air, following the path the girl had taken.

He ate his breakfast and fed his horse before he left the empty clearing in the Great Forest and rode back to the Crones' castle to celebrate Christmas Day with them.

71

Winter left the old house and began to take its turn again with the other seasons. Spring came. The grass turned green, and the birds built nests and raised noisy families under the eaves of the old house. Summer followed spring, bringing heat and all manner of wild things. Wild flowers bloomed in the fields; berry bushes bore fruit. Red roses bloomed over the porch.

But now, the door hinges of the old house were oiled, the windows were clean and bright, and the old porch swing gleamed with a new coat of white paint. Cats and other animals lounged among the clay flower pots on the porch.

The paper the young woman had found in the rose paper magic box was the deed to the old house; once sheltered in the old rose paper box, now it lay under glass on the dresser top in her mother's old bedroom, her bedroom now.

Sometimes at night, the moon peeked through the mended, whispering lace curtains and stroked the rose paper magic box and the paper on the dresser with moonlight before bathing the sleeping face of the young woman with moon glow. The moon, in its wisdom, knew it would be there to caress that same face when it grew old, too.

A hunter passing through the Great Forest on a cold winter's day near Christmas, came across a little empty hut. Magic dwelt therein, for fresh red roses had climbed all around the door and over the roof. Their scent was wild and sweet; they reminded him of something that couldn't be conquered. He took off his cap and stared at the hut while he measured the magic before him.

He recalled a story he had heard about the Great Forest and its mysterious doings.

It was told that animals living in the Great Forest gathered in a magic clearing each Christmas Eve, where they were fed and kept safe all through the night by two women, one young and one old, a mother and daughter, who both bore an enduring love of red roses and the warm, red courage they wrought.

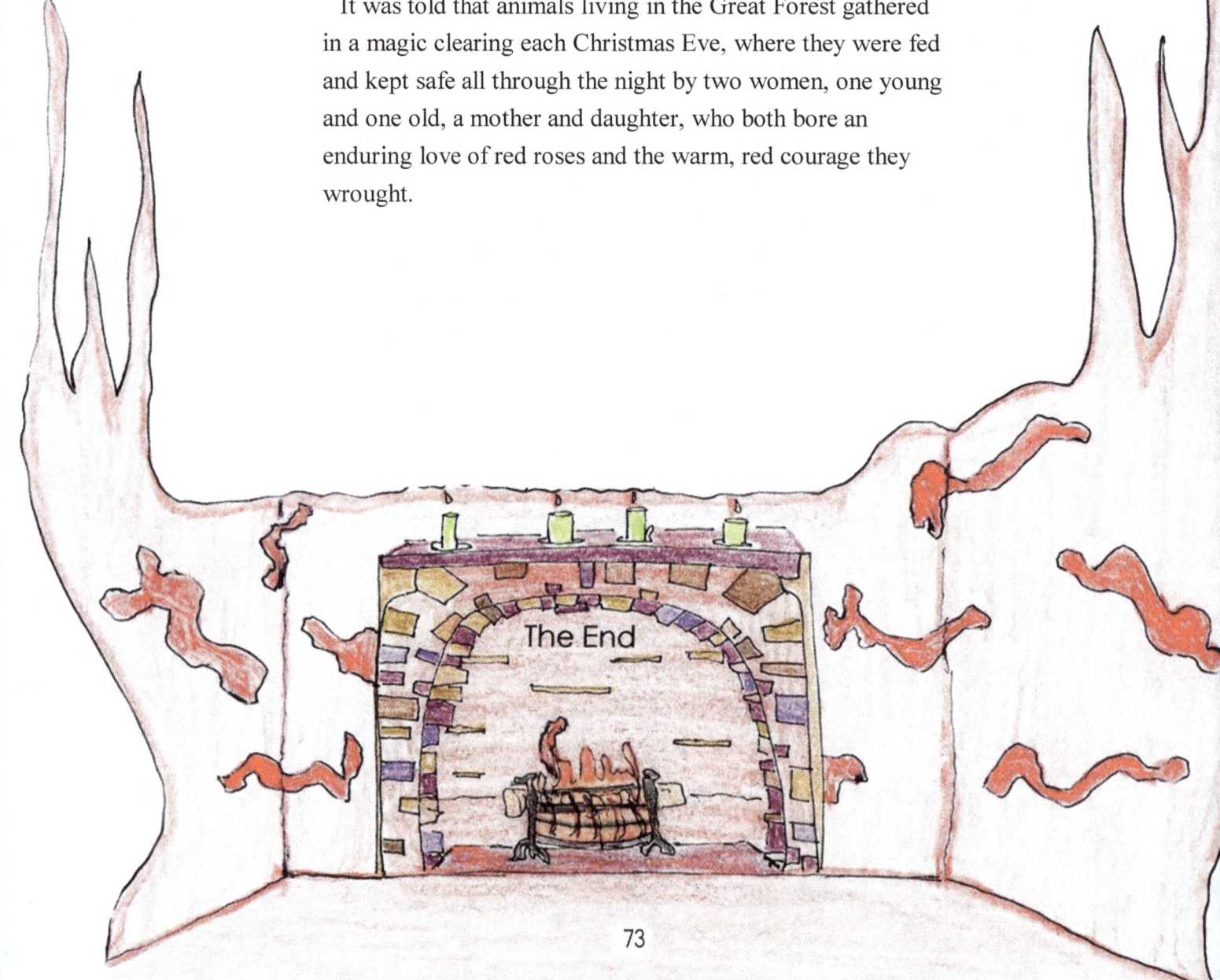

The End

5 The Smile so Snug in an Old Magic Box

From "Once Upon a Time,"

'Twas the past,
that held them fast,
until the forces of old
made them bold,
and forthwith, anew…

74

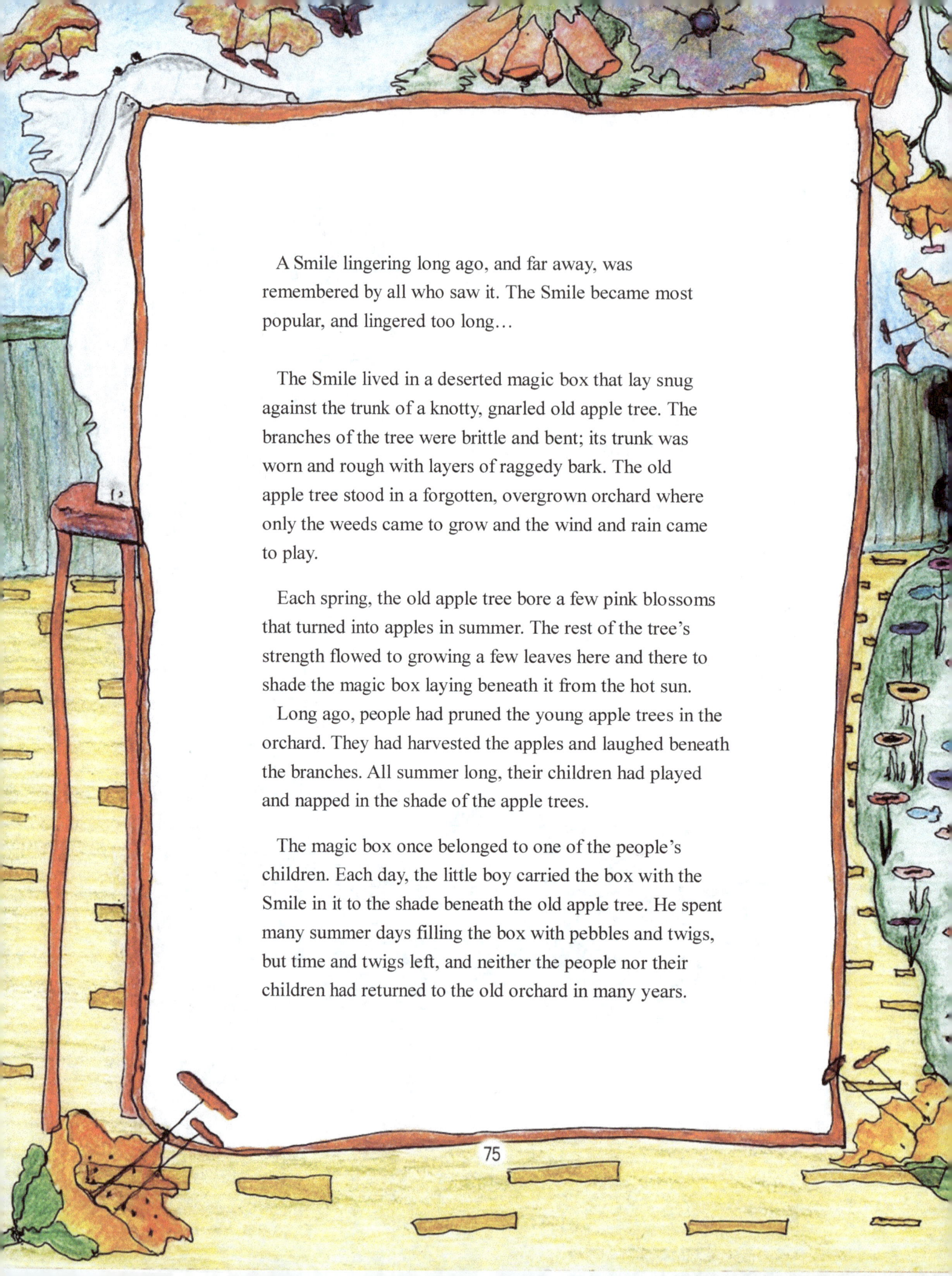

A Smile lingering long ago, and far away, was remembered by all who saw it. The Smile became most popular, and lingered too long…

The Smile lived in a deserted magic box that lay snug against the trunk of a knotty, gnarled old apple tree. The branches of the tree were brittle and bent; its trunk was worn and rough with layers of raggedy bark. The old apple tree stood in a forgotten, overgrown orchard where only the weeds came to grow and the wind and rain came to play.

Each spring, the old apple tree bore a few pink blossoms that turned into apples in summer. The rest of the tree's strength flowed to growing a few leaves here and there to shade the magic box laying beneath it from the hot sun.

Long ago, people had pruned the young apple trees in the orchard. They had harvested the apples and laughed beneath the branches. All summer long, their children had played and napped in the shade of the apple trees.

The magic box once belonged to one of the people's children. Each day, the little boy carried the box with the Smile in it to the shade beneath the old apple tree. He spent many summer days filling the box with pebbles and twigs, but time and twigs left, and neither the people nor their children had returned to the old orchard in many years.

The old box lay up against the trunk of the old apple tree, alone and empty, except for a few twigs and pebbles and the Smile that had lingered there too long.

The wind played in the orchard; the sun rose and set. Rains wet the orchard with life-giving water; birds nested in the branches and taught their babies to fly away. Life went on with its many cycles, but no people came to the orchard.

But the Smile had faith! It believed that someday, it would fly out of the magic box and be seen again! And, oh, how it would shine! Day after day, and year after year, the Smile practiced for the moment when it would be found once again.

And so, the seasons came and went in the orchard. The wind carried stories of the life outside the orchard to the eager apple tree and the magic box. It told of places and people and things. It told of scents, and colors and noises. And so, the old apple tree and the Smile and the twigs and pebbles in the box stayed fairly content. Their home was their home, and there was nothing to do about it, but wait and hope that a time might come that freed them from the orchard.

Autumn followed summer. The autumn wind was cool and lofty and very busy. It tugged the leaves off the trees in the orchard and scaled their bark with short, sharp gusts.

Fall winds banked the leaves against the tree trunks and whirled through the tall grass, bending it over so the ground would not crack open when the ice of winter froze it.

Winter came, layering snow over the apple tree and the magic box. Winter whispered to the old apple tree and the magic box, telling stories of ice floes, snow palaces, and of children skating to and fro on ponds.

Spring brought rain and warm, curling air that melted snow's blanket. The rain murmured and pattered and fell on the apple trees and ground, soaking into their roots, waking them up for another year of apple growing.

The bold, hot sun strolled through the orchard all summer long, tossing little breezes here and there just as it pleased, causing the magic box to imagine it heard a certain child's laughing voice once again.

For a long time, the Smile lived alone in the magic box. Then Grimaces and Frowns started moving in, just a few at a time. The Smile ignored them, and kept practicing for the day it would be found again.

Every now and then, when the wind passed through the old orchard, it caught the lid of the magic box and held it open just long enough for the Smile to jump out and beam its dazzling self in all directions. The wind always held the lid open just long enough to let the Smile come out and go back in. Then it raced away before the Grimaces and Frowns could take it to task for closing the lid before they could come out, too.

After all, the Grimaces and Frowns grumbled to themselves, they had been living in the magic box quite a long time, too! Although the Smile had been there first, the Grimaces and Frowns wanted to come out and be special, too.

The Shrugs that had moved in after the Grimaces and Frowns didn't care one way or the other when the Grimaces and Frowns asked their opinion of the situation. They just shrugged, because that's what Shrugs do.

After a while, the Grimaces and Frowns decided they'd endured enough of the Smile and the wind's errant ways. Something had to be done; the situation demanded to be put on a schedule. With this goal in mind, they formed a committee and held meetings, elected officers, took notes, decoded deductions, and came up with a plan. The shrugs said, "Sure." then shrugged.

One day, when the sky was dull, and the rain came and went in the orchard, the Grimaces and Frowns heard the wind blowing outside the magic box. It was getting ready to let the Smile out for its exercise.

Quickly they gathered together and set out on their journey. With determination and a large map, they climbed and hiked, hoping to reach the top of the magic box before the wind stopped blowing.

After climbing a long time, they lost their way; The Grimaces and Frowns blazed a new trail to Despair, a place they had never visited before. Like the Shrugs, Despair was no help at all to the wandering Grimaces and Frowns. In fact, while the Shrugs were in Despair, nobody did anything.

Despair moaned and groaned and wailed and owned screaming goats who danced by moats. Despair was dark, dense, and drippy. Moisture and slow-moving vapors floated in the wet air. Hiding everywhere were small moans, misty mutters, and sagging sighs. The Grimaces discovered, to their chagrin, that the Shrugs had relatives living in Despair and all those kin liked to bunch together and roam around aimlessly.

The Grimaces and Frowns visited with the others silently and politely, but in a very short time, they became moody and depressed, and trudged back to their home deep in the magic box. Ah, but a bunch of the small Moans, little Mutters and Heaving sighs from despair followed them home! What to do with them?

The Grimaces and Frowns, for all their no, no, non-sense, were a very silent and polite bunch, and very respectful of the rights of others. They noticed they were being followed, and in self-defense, as soon as they got home, they hastily built a small, but grand motel for the Moans, Mutters, and Sighs. They built the small, but grand motel far away from where they themselves lived, so they wouldn't have to listen to the newcomers while they visited with their relatives.

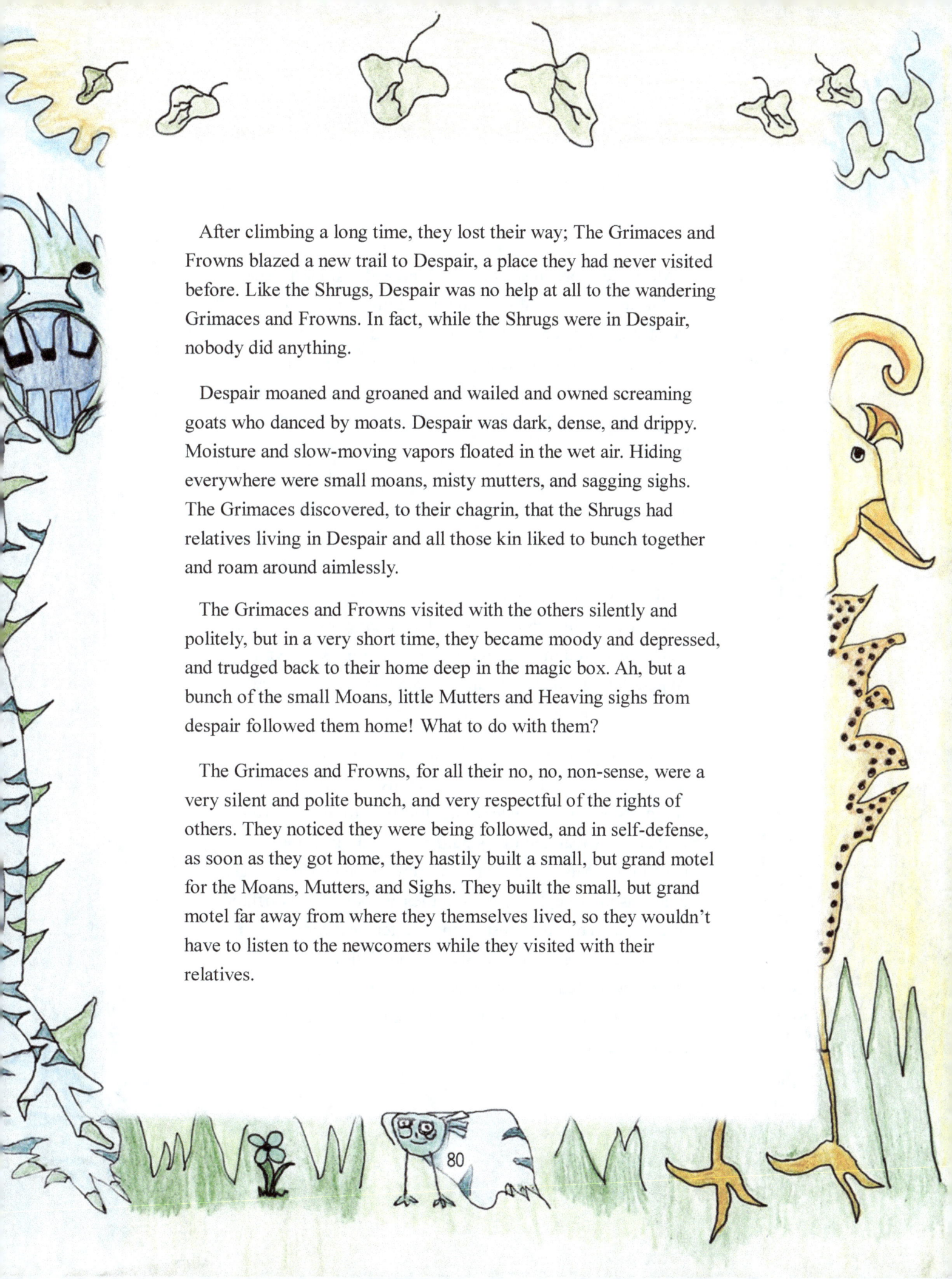

After a few days rest from climbing and visiting Despair, and from hastily building a small, but grand motel, the exhausted Grimaces and Frowns realized they needed to formulate a new plan. They took more notes and wrote more decoded deductions of an even more singular nature; they scratched and penciled until they had a new plan in place.

One day, they heard the wind blowing outside the box again, and they set out on their second journey. That time, they accidently blazed a trail over to Anger. Anger? Yes, Anger was living in the box, too, and it exercised a lot while waiting to come out of the box and become a star. Anger was thrifty, short tempered, and hot. Howls and yells and shouts lived there. After a short but polite visit with Anger, during which they all sweated a lot, the Grimaces and Frowns headed home again.

But a gaggle of Shouts, Yells, and Howls followed them, forcing the silent Grimaces and Frowns to hastily build another small, but grander motel for them to live in, even farther away than the first small, but grand motel they'd built for the Mutters and Moans from Despair. After the last twig was in place, they checked their work and went off to rest again. While they rested, the Mutters and Moans from Despair, and the Sighs and Shouts and Yells and Howls from Anger became well acquainted with each other. They visited back and forth in their small, but grand motels, fading in and out of the walls.

After they grew tired of scaring each other, they held camp outs, sing alongs, picnics, and late-night séances. Their calamitous noise filled the air day and night, except for a tiny slice of the early morning hours when they all slept. The Grimaces and Frowns, having always been a polite and silent bunch, held secret, desperate meetings in the early morning hours while the noisy motel occupants slept. Their new plan was to visit the Smile, whom none of them knew very well.

They needed an introduction, so they invited a Soothsayer, a skilled Prophet of Doom, Gloom, and Reconciliation to lead them to the Smile's home. The Prophet would, of course, introduce them, and present their case to the Smile.

They chose a venerable rebel elder who had wandered into their area not long ago, partly because he was the only one they could find. Being an aged rebel Prophet, he was highly skilled in scoffing, piffling, napping, and various other aged rebel activities.

The Prophet was gnarled and bent and very noisy. He had a long, pointed beard he often tripped over. His worn robe held endless secret pockets filled with magic tools he had collected over his many years. The tools clanked and clattered with every step he took. When he tripped over his beard, the tools clunked and thunked and banged and binged

with long lasting echoes, causing him to

resort to extra verbiage and sneezing.

Early one morning, while everyone living in the small, but grand motels was sleeping, the committee of Grimaces and Frowns set out on their third journey with the Prophet of Doom, Gloom, and Reconciliation leading the way. He carried a note of compromise and vigorously waved a white flag in front of him.

The Grimaces and Frowns had taken precautions. They had lined his pockets with cotton and tucked the end of his long beard under his wide black belt; they planned to keep him silent, even if his beard came out of his belt and he tripped over it.

But alas! At the last minute, everyone sleeping in the small but grand motels woke up and heard them leaving. They jumped out of their sleeping places and followed after the Prophet and the Grimaces and Frowns.

The Grimaces and Frowns ignored them and kept marching grimly forward. There was not going to be plan four! This was it!

They walked and climbed towards the top of the magic box, where legend said the Smile lived.

At last, the Prophet stopped and pointed towards the lid high above them. Small beams of sunlight filtered down through the thin cracks in the lid and almost touched them. They stood in the dim darkness, looking up. A few of them remembered the light; many of them had never seen it before.

They all sat down quietly to eat and rest while the Prophet paced back and forth. He took scrolls and measuring devices out of his pockets and consulted them. He pointed the measuring devices at the beams of light filtering down through the lid and scribbled numbers and equations on papers. He unfurled his long beard from his wide, black belt and rubbed it. He began to pace again but tripped over his beard and fell on his devices, causing him to sneeze and piffle.

He got back on his feet, but after a while, he stopped and yawned. It was close to his nap time, and he never liked to miss his nap. Besides loving naps, he secretly suspected they would never find the Smile.

It was a lost cause, a thing he didn't put up with, for all his causes had been found, groomed, and stayed tucked snug in their beds. It was time to rebel, a thing he loved to do. What was there to lose? He tucked his beard back into his wide black belt and tossed the white flag and the note of compromise high up in the air. Then he raised both hands towards the tiny, shiny beams of light above them and shouted in his most thunderous voice,

"Stand up! It's time to be a star! Right here and now, be the star you have always wanted to be!"

The Grimaces and Frowns stretched themselves into mighty Grimaces and huge Frowns. The Shrugs shrugged as substantially as they could. The Mutters and Moans, Sighs and Shouts, Yells and Howls did their very best. They shuddered and screamed and wailed. They stomped and gestured and bellowed. They became more and more creative and noisier and louder as the clamor mounted.

The Prophet of Doom and Gloom and Reconciliation happily threw lightning bolts thither and yon, forcing all of them to dance and scream even more shrilly and louder. The lid of the old magic box creaked and groaned from the pressure building inside it.

At last, the lid flew open. The Smile, who had been hiding in a dark corner underneath the lid, rushed out of the box and hid behind the trunk of the old apple tree.

With pomp and circumstance, the Prophet led the way out of the magic box. Everyone in the box followed him out. The box was empty. For hours they displayed their finest talents in the shade under the apple tree. Finally, they began to laugh and turn cartwheels and play games of tag with each other in the long grass under the tree. After they wore themselves out, they all settled by the roots of the tree and napped and watched the sun begin to go down behind the orchard. It was time for them to decide whether to stay or go.

The Wails and Moans decided to visit relatives who conducted nightly tours of ghost ships in the warm, wet tropics. They looked forward to a vacation after all they had been through. They went back inside the deserted magic box and packed their suitcases. Then they thanked everyone and went their way.

The Mutters and Shudders decided to search out quiet, shady, tree lined lanes in deep, dark woods, so they could demonstrate their unique skills to unsuspecting travelers.

The Shouts and Howls decided to join a carnival. They would have their own haunted house on wheels and would tour the world. There would always be new people to scare. What's more, they would get paid for scaring them!

The silent Grimaces and Frowns decided to travel the world and frequent ancient libraries and soothing art galleries for a while. They needed some peace and quiet and cultured surroundings to heal their frazzled nerves. The Shrugs decided to go with them.

After everyone had decided where they were going, they packed their things and gathered in the tall grass under the old apple tree to say goodbye to each other. As each one left, the Prophet handed them a small pebble or a twig that the magic box's boy had left in it. He once had loved the box, you see.

After everyone was gone, the Prophet handed the pouch containing the last few twigs and pebbles to the Smile, and went his own way, clanging and banging along.

The Smile, a few small Sighs and one Tear
climbed back into the old magic box. They opened
the pouch and scattered the leftover twigs and
pebbles on the bottom of the box before they made
themselves a new place to curl up and fall asleep.
The sun set over the old apple orchard. The
curious wind wandered through the orchard and
riffled through the branches of the old apple tree.
It noticed the lid of the box was open, and swept
down and closed it. Once more, the box sat in
silence under the apple tree…

Now we come to the next part, in which the
Smile, the few small Sighs, and the one Tear
still living in the box, at last set out on their own
adventures…

87

Fall came again, and the few apples and leaves on the trees in the orchard fell to the ground. The grass growing around the magic box grew thin and brittle.

The cool wind rustled through the branches of the apple trees and forgot to open the lid of the old magic box. Soon, winter layered the tree branches and the ground of the old orchard with a blanket of snow.

On a cold, still night, when the sky was dark and crowded with shining stars, the old magic box cracked open from the cold.

The Smile, the few small Sighs, and the single Tear fell out into the snow. They climbed back into the box, but the cold had broken it apart, and it was much too cold for them to stay inside. It was time for them to move on.

The Smile gathered the last few pebbles and twigs from the bottom of the box and put them into the pouch again. Then all of them climbed out of the box for the last time, and stood in the frosty night air.

The Smile climbed up in the old apple tree to see which way they should go. It saw lights off in the distance and flew down to tell the others what it had seen. The Smile clutched the pouch tightly as they set out on their journey towards the distant lights. It took them a long time to climb up and down the high snowdrifts in the orchard.

At last they came to the fence enclosing the old orchard. Beyond it were the lights the Smile had seen. They peeked around the side of a fence post and saw a street. On the other side of the street was a sidewalk, and past it were the beautiful lights that were their destination. The lights glowed from a green tree that stood in front of a house in a snow-covered yard. The wind carried the scent of the Christmas tree across the street to them. The smell was sharp and sweet, and beckoned to them.

They crept around the fencepost and started climbing down the steep snow that had drifted up against the post. Suddenly, they were scooped up in a large shovel and tossed across the street. They flew through the air, past the sidewalk, and landed underneath the green tree flickering with lights. The Smile, the few small Sighs and the one Tear climbed up among the glowing lights on the branches and looked around. The lights were bright and warm, and they were so cold and so tired from their long journey!

Each of the weary little travelers picked out a light and snuggled up to its warmth. Soon, they were all fast asleep. Snowflakes began drifting down. A group of people gathered beneath the tree and began singing Christmas carols.

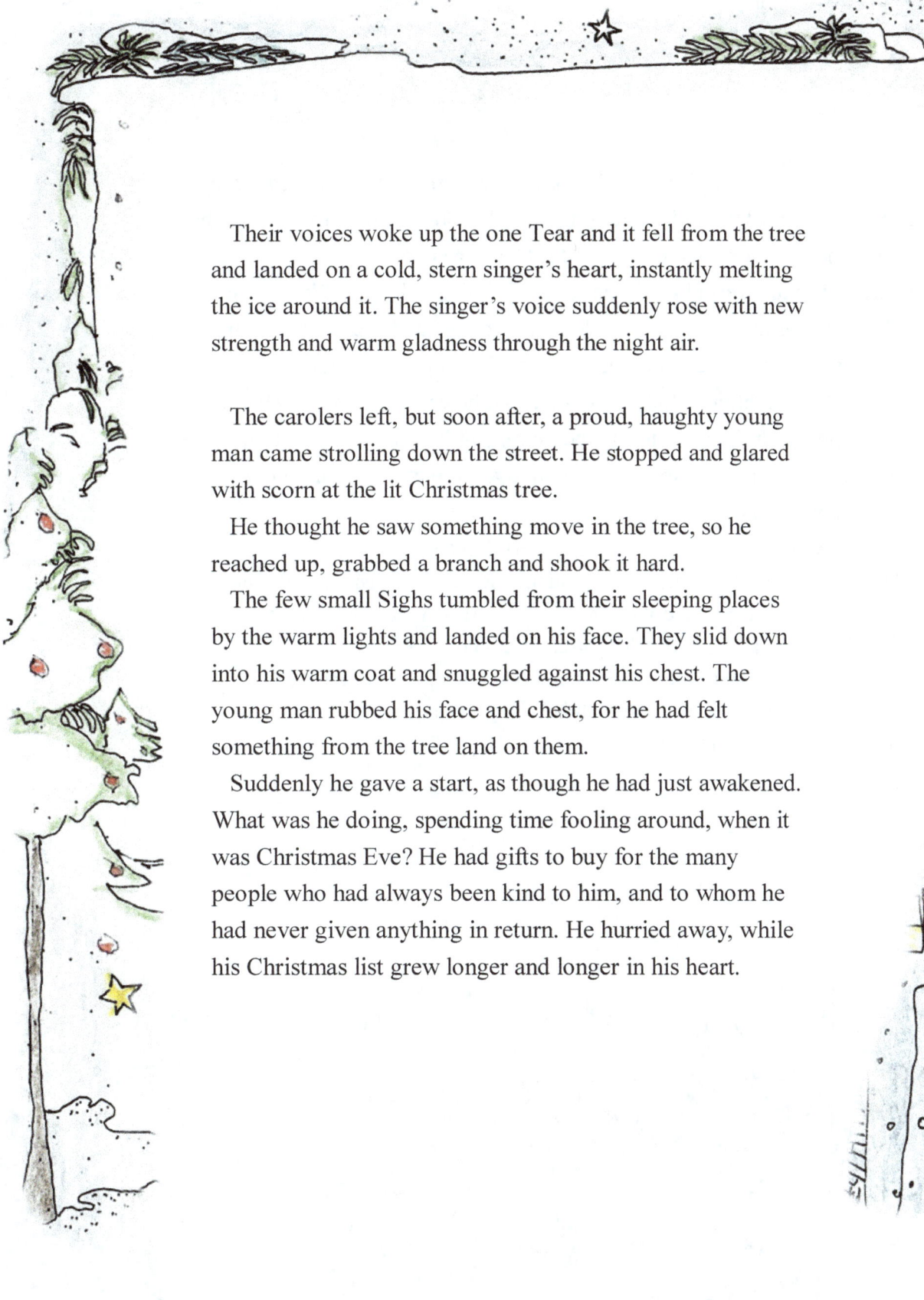

Their voices woke up the one Tear and it fell from the tree and landed on a cold, stern singer's heart, instantly melting the ice around it. The singer's voice suddenly rose with new strength and warm gladness through the night air.

The carolers left, but soon after, a proud, haughty young man came strolling down the street. He stopped and glared with scorn at the lit Christmas tree.

He thought he saw something move in the tree, so he reached up, grabbed a branch and shook it hard.

The few small Sighs tumbled from their sleeping places by the warm lights and landed on his face. They slid down into his warm coat and snuggled against his chest. The young man rubbed his face and chest, for he had felt something from the tree land on them.

Suddenly he gave a start, as though he had just awakened. What was he doing, spending time fooling around, when it was Christmas Eve? He had gifts to buy for the many people who had always been kind to him, and to whom he had never given anything in return. He hurried away, while his Christmas list grew longer and longer in his heart.

The Smile slept on while people passed back and forth underneath the tree. The hour grew later and later until finally, the old man who lived in the house behind the tree came out to turn off his Christmas lights.

As soon as the warm lights went off, the Smile woke up. It looked around, and saw it was all alone. The Smile looked down, and seeing the old man standing under the tree, it grabbed the pouch and jumped out of the tree. The old man felt something land on his shoe and he bent over to see what it was. The Smile was holding on to his shoe lace, smiling mightily up at him. The old man stared down at the Smile, then bent over to pick up the little pouch laying in the snow by his shoe.

"Well, well, and so then," he said. "What have we got here?"
He straightened and opened the pouch. He reached inside, took out a tiny pebble and a twig and looked them over with wonder and delight.

"Well, well, and so...I'd forgotten," he said.

He grinned down at the Smile, then he laughed. At that moment, the Smile heard the very same child's laughter it had yearned to hear from so long ago.

Suddenly, the old man danced a little jig in the snow. The Smile flew off his shoe and landed amid a group of people on their way to the church around the corner for the midnight Christmas caroling.

They invited the old man to go with them, and as he made his way up the porch steps to get his coat, he decided to turn the Christmas tree lights on again and leave them on all night. Soon he joined the people waiting for him, and they walked down the street. The Smile loved being in the crowd of people. It flashed in and out and flew all around them as they entered the church. Pretty soon, lulled by the warmth of the church, the Smile grew sleepy again. It yawned and flew onto the old man's coat where it snuggled up under his collar and fell asleep.

Outside, a few snowflakes drifted down in the late night stillness. The lights on the Christmas tree made pools of bright, soft color. No one was there to notice the Box Keeper who stopped, laid down his snow shovel and searched carefully through the tree's branches. When he was satisfied that the Smile, the Tear and the Sighs were gone, he picked up his snow shovel, began whistling, and strolled away.

The End

6. The Box and the Beautiful Green Bottle

From a work in progress, "A Rhyme in Time,"

"Two trees grew tall, their boughs touched close
their young leaves green and fair
burnished to gold in winter air.
Sleep winter said. Sleep.
The tree's bare limbs clicked against each other,
rhyme for rime; they stood together in the falling
snow covering the golden earth."

A long time ago, when magic rings were woven from tall, green grasses growing on the banks of forgotten streams, in the Kingdom of true Believers in Imagination, an old magic box lay near the edge of such a stream. The old box did not remember how it came to be there, it only knew it had been there a long time. As quickly as the old magic box came to rest there, grass grew tall around it, capturing it within its thin, deep roots, holding on to it until the box couldn't move any more.

Two tall oak trees stood near the stream bank. In summer, they shaded the old magic box from the hot sun. The box sat in solemn silence, watching the life that flowed by in the forgotten stream.

Then one spring day, a wind whipped, pounding rain whirled and twirled an old green bottle with a cork in its top down the stream. Inside the bottle was a scrap of yellowed paper and a few other things. Broken branches already bent over the stream caught the green bottle and tossed it up on the creek bank. The bottle rolled along until it got caught in the grass that lay near the old magic box.

The seasons came and went while the old box and the green bottle rested silently near each other until another spring storm came and broke the old bottle loose from the twisted grass it was caught in. The green bottle bumped up against the old box and rolled to a stop a short distance away. The bump startled the box and it woke up from the dream it was having. In the dream, a young man held the box in his hands. He was walking with a lovely girl, dressed in white, under two young oak trees.

The box wondered what had bumped into it and its curiosity grew. It began making creaking, questioning noises. The green bottle heard the noises the box made, but it could not answer because it had a cork in its top.

After a while, the box gave up and became silent again. But things had changed. The box and the bottle shared each other's silent presence, and neither of them was quite as lonely as they had been before. The box yearned to speak to the new other and wanted to keep it company, but it couldn't. It was almost in pieces, for it had sat in the grasses on the stream bank too long.

The Kingdom's Box Keepers learned of the box's plight, and set out to find the forgotten old magic box. They felt the yearnings coming from it, and searched for it everywhere. As they searched, the yearnings and dreams from the box grew weaker and weaker. The Box Keepers did not find it for many days and weeks.

Then one day, they came across an old woman sitting on the bank of a forgotten stream. She wore a crown of flowers in her white hair, and she was braiding more magic crowns from the tall, green grass growing at the streams edge. As the Box Keepers drew closer, she raised her hand and pointed at the two tall oak trees in the distance. Then she stood up and disappeared.

A short time later, the Box Keepers stood under the two oak trees that bordered the stream. The Box Keepers searched until they found the box and bottle resting near each other in the tall grass close to the stream's edge.

The Box Keepers returned to their horses and donned their finest clothes and carried their lutes and flutes over to the box and bottle. They sat down near them and played their instruments. When they stopped, one of them began to tell a story.

The box heard their voices and was soon wide awake. With a great deal of effort, it managed to lift a corner of its lid a wee, tiny bit. The Box Keeper stopped his story and smiled down at the old box. "Hello. We've come to visit you," he said.

The old box had a few wispy threads of memory left in it. On hearing the Box Keepers' tunes, the threads busily brushed up on their manners and welcomed their guests.

The beautiful green bottle lay silently beside the box. It had much to say, much to ask, but it could do neither, because it had a cork in its top and could not speak. Still, it listened to the Box Keepers' music and it felt the brushing up of manners and the welcome from the box.

The Box Keepers stayed. They set up camp. They cooked beans and biscuits and played more music for the box and bottle. Deep into the darkness of the starry nights, they shared battle shouts, sweet, cool songs, and cold, chilling mystery stories with the box and bottle. They shared stories of the past, and what the Kingdom of True Believers in Imagination was like at the beginning of long ago, when the old, abandoned shoe box factory located on the edge of a big city became their secret, magical Kingdom.

One day, as they camped by the box and the bottle, the Box Keepers told them a story about a young boy and his childhood sweetheart, and how one summer, they planted the two oak trees that shaded the box and bottle now, on the edge of the forgotten stream.

As often happens in such matters, the day came when the Box Keepers had to leave the box and bottle alone again. The box was sad, but it felt content, even though it knew it was near its end; after all, the Box Keepers had helped it remember most of its life story. It could not have asked for more. The green bottle had nothing to say for it still had a cork in its top.

The Box Keepers left. Winter came again. One cold day, an old man walked slowly towards the two oak trees. Though he was white haired and bent from age, the two oaks remembered him. They clicked their branches together in delighted unison when he walked under them. The old man smiled up at them before he went to find the box.

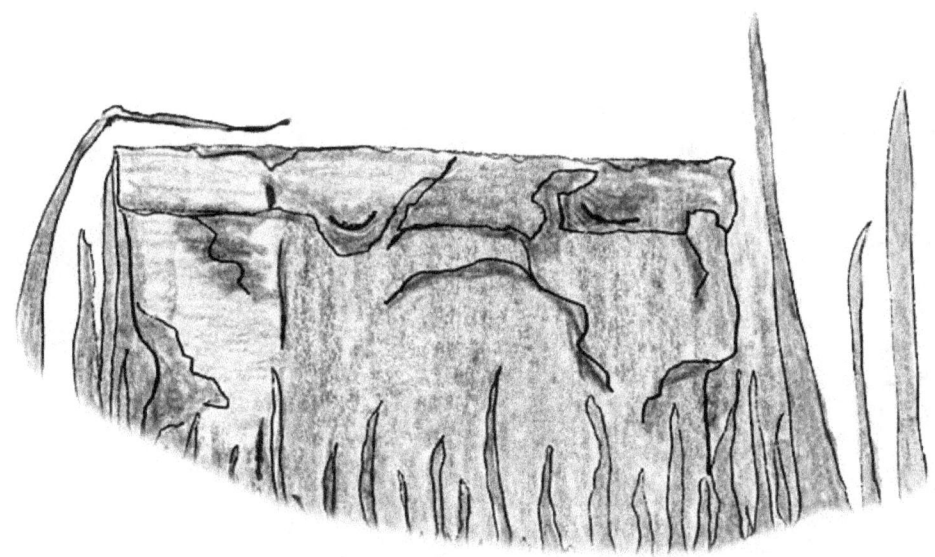

Searching through the tall grass, he bent down and ran his fingers across the top of the old box. The two trees watched while he knelt and carefully loosened the grass around the box and picked it up. Just as he stood up, holding the box in his hands, the icy, hungry fingers of a gust of wintery wind grabbed at the box. The old man tried to protect the box from the wind, but it crumbled to pieces in his hands.

The cold, cruel wind grabbed pieces from him and scattered them through the winter air. The old man shook his head in sorrow and carefully laid the few pieces of the box left in his hands back on the ground where the box had lain for so many years. When he stood up, he noticed the beautiful green bottle. He picked it up and brushed it off and looked at it curiously. The bare branches of the two trees clicked against each other again as he walked beneath them, carrying the old green bottle away.

A few days later, the old man was sitting near the fireplace in his favorite chair, watching the falling snow through the window, remembering Christmases past. His generations were gathered, laughing and talking around the large, stately Christmas tree at the other end of the room. The tree was filled with ornaments the hands and hearts his generations had made over the years; each of them examined their ornaments with delight.

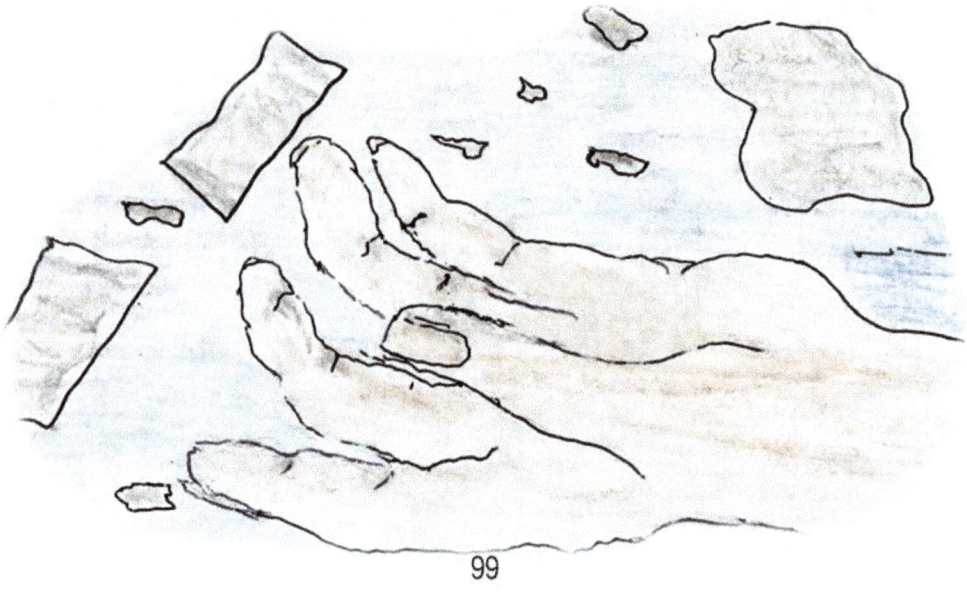

He waited until they were all busy opening the gifts stacked beneath the tree before he carefully withdrew the beautiful, old green bottle from its hiding place. He lifted the bottle and peered at the yellowed scrap of paper inside it. He sighed, remembering how, long ago, a hasty youth had placed a note inside a green bottle and flung it into a stream. As the bottle bobbed upright in the water, the youth had sped away on a whim, to the four corners of the earth. His once auburn hair had flown in the wind back then; now it was white and gleamed in the firelight.

The old man tugged the cork out of the bottle and poured the contents out on the blanket covering his lap. Small voices poured out of the bottle, humming song from his tender youth. Memories poured out of the top of the bottle, followed by pieces of how the future could be, came to be, and was.

He picked up the folded scrap of yellowed paper, read the scrawled note of his youthful, hasty leaving of long ago. He closed his eyes and thought about love and a girl who wore white and intricate crowns of braided grasses in brown hair. He opened his eyes, and there she stood, wearing a white dress, a crown of paper made by a great-grandchild on her white hair.

He reached for her hand and she smiled at his touch. Later, they stood before their fireplace alone, singing Christmas carols to welcome in the everlasting love that shines warm and sweet throughout all of life, and past life and into forever, while outside, the cold, hungry wind searched the crevices of their house for entry.

The End

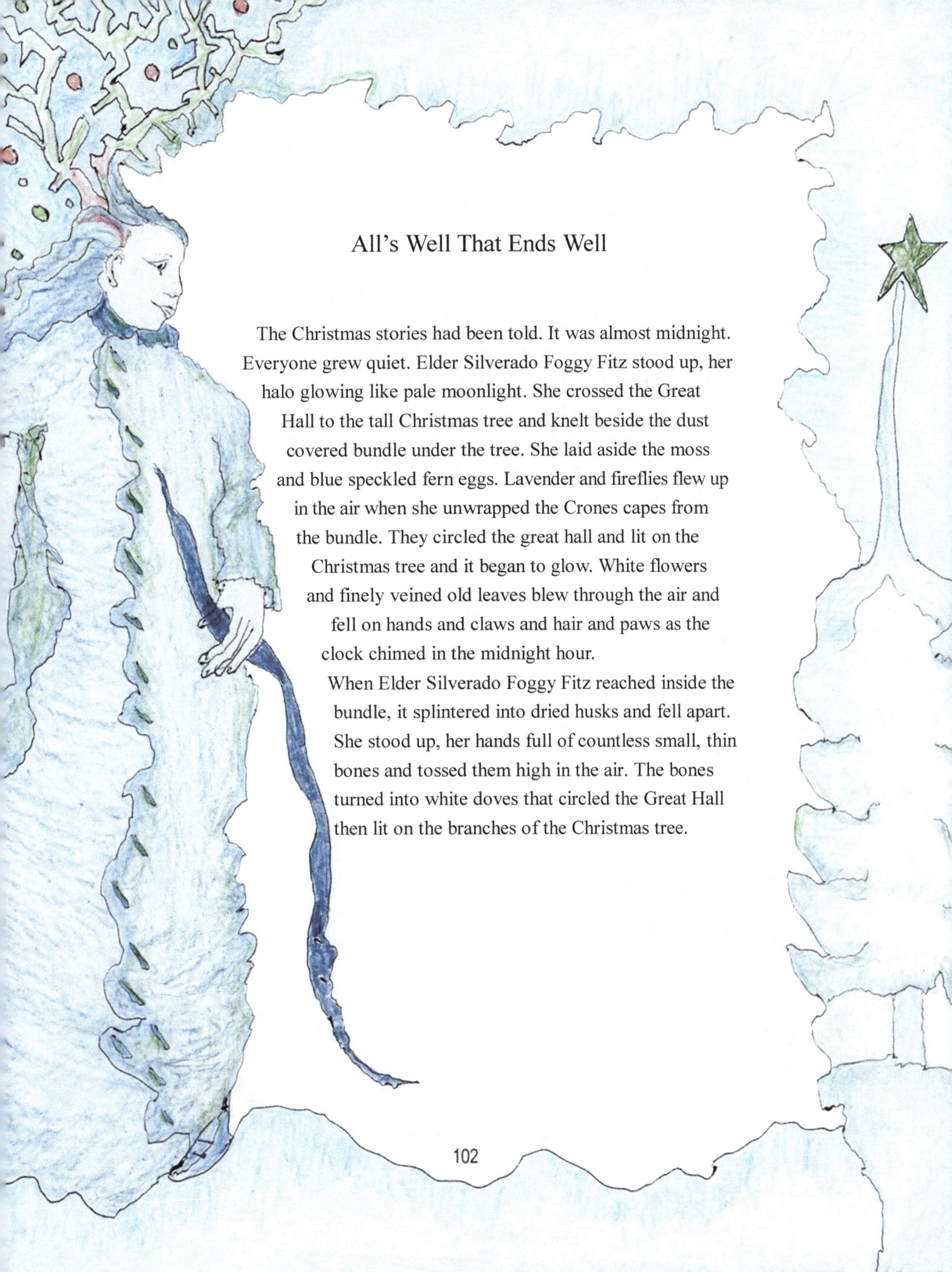

All's Well That Ends Well

The Christmas stories had been told. It was almost midnight.
Everyone grew quiet. Elder Silverado Foggy Fitz stood up, her
halo glowing like pale moonlight. She crossed the Great
Hall to the tall Christmas tree and knelt beside the dust
covered bundle under the tree. She laid aside the moss
and blue speckled fern eggs. Lavender and fireflies flew up
in the air when she unwrapped the Crones capes from
the bundle. They circled the great hall and lit on the
Christmas tree and it began to glow. White flowers
and finely veined old leaves blew through the air and
fell on hands and claws and hair and paws as the
clock chimed in the midnight hour.

When Elder Silverado Foggy Fitz reached inside the
bundle, it splintered into dried husks and fell apart.
She stood up, her hands full of countless small, thin
bones and tossed them high in the air. The bones
turned into white doves that circled the Great Hall
then lit on the branches of the Christmas tree.

102

Like the smoothest, warmest of honey, an ancient peace, mightily sought and hard won, a peace wise in the ways of boys and girls and Box Keepers and Crones and Others, poured over everyone gathered in the Great Hall. Outside the Crones' castle, the falling snow reflected the glow of peace within. The windows and doors of the castle flew open. Snow and light and wind blew in and lifted up the gift of Peace and carried it out of the castle. The rusty doors of the old, abandoned shoe box factory opened, and the snow and light danced through them, carrying the gift of Peace out into the world. After a while, the light dimmed and the rusty doors of the old abandoned shoebox factory closed again.

The End

103

From the quill, ink and parchment of Patsy Stanley,
A Christmas Goodnight.

When the last story was told,
the Bards of old,
and the Box Keepers, Crones, and Others,
went off to their beds to get some rest,
and to sleep beneath their covers.
The candles shone bright,
all through the night,
in the castle still and tall,
as throughout the world,
boys and girls were gifted,
one and all. As the new dawn arose,
they donned their robes,
and went to the Christmas tree singing,
and the gifts, glad and bright,
were claimed by their hands,
as the bells throughout the land were ringing.

Merry Christmas, one and all!"